INVINCIBLE SUMMER

HANNAH MOSKOWITZ

SIMON PULSE

NEW YORK   LONDON   TORONTO   SYDNEY

This book is a work of fiction. Any references to historical events, real people, or real locales are used fictitiously. Other names, characters, places, and incidents are the product of the author's imagination, and any resemblance to actual events or locales or persons, living or dead, is entirely coincidental.

SIMON PULSE

An imprint of Simon & Schuster Children's Publishing Division

1230 Avenue of the Americas, New York, NY 10020

First Simon Pulse paperback edition April 2011

Copyright © 2011 by Hannah Moskowitz

All rights reserved, including the right of reproduction in whole or in part in any form.

SIMON PULSE and colophon are registered trademarks of Simon & Schuster, Inc.

For information about special discounts for bulk purchases, please contact Simon & Schuster Special Sales at 1-866-506-1949 or business@simonandschuster.com.

The Simon & Schuster Speakers Bureau can bring authors to your live event. For more information or to book an event contact the Simon & Schuster Speakers Bureau at 1-866-248-3049 or visit our website at www.simonspeakers.com.

Designed by Mike Rosamilia

The text of this book was set in Berling LT Std.

Manufactured in the United States of America

2 4 6 8 10 9 7 5 3 1

Library of Congress Control Number 2010014825

ISBN 978-1-4424-0751-0

ISBN 978-1-4424-0752-7 (eBook)

INVINCIBLE SUMMER

ALSO BY
HANNAH MOSKOWITZ:

Break

To my family, invincibly

15TH SUMMER

ONE

Gideon keeps falling down.

He and Claudia slipped outside to the beach and were out there for at least ten minutes before my parents or Noah or I noticed they were gone. They're greasy and gritty now with sand and seawater, so there's no point in dragging them back inside and getting everything dirty our first night here, plus none of us feel like putting in the effort to chase them. My mother, who's a little too old and way too pregnant to run around outside and parent them hands-on like she used to, drifts to the porch off the first floor to watch them and make sure they don't kill themselves, one hand on her stomach, one on the railing.

Noah and I linger by the windows on the other side of the family room, our foreheads pressed against the glass. We're moaning every time we see a particularly good wave roll by and looking at each other—maybe we should go out? Maybe we can? No.

Outside, Claudia is laughing loudly enough for us to hear. She always says she's way too old to play with Gideon, and she's not going to, no way, and if we want a babysitter, we can pay her. But she always ends up playing with him anyway, at least when we're here. Here no one is too old. Except Mom and Dad. And Claudia and Gideon are the two youngest, so they get shoved together and there is no way to avoid it, even though Claudia's eleven and Gideon's barely six.

Dad says, "Aren't you two going out?"

We can't. Even though there's sand stuck to our feet from the walk from the car, up the stairs, inside, and back, and back, and back, while we hauled in suitcases. Even though the carpet smells like old sunscreen. Noah and I know that it isn't quite summer. Not yet. Summer can't start at night, first of all, and it definitely can't start before we see the SUV roll up outside the Hathaways' beach house. And until it comes, we'll wait here. That's tradition, and Noah and I do not kill tradition. If we get here before the Hathaways, we wait.

Dad says, "You boys are sticks in the mud."

"Heathen," Noah mutters.

Dad's not pregnant, but he acts like he is, complaining that he's so tired from the drive, that he needs to put his feet up. He sits on the scratchy couch—the one with years of our sand embedded between the cushions—and complains, like every year, that the renters have moved the furniture.

We're totally not listening.

"Boys," he says. "They're probably not coming until tomorrow."

"They always come the same day we do," I say.

Dad says, "You'd be able to hear the car from the beach. Go outside and make sure Gideon doesn't get dizzy."

Making sure Gideon doesn't get dizzy is one of our family duties, along with *getting Mom's slippers, thinking of a name for Chase's song, washing the makeup off your sister's face are you kidding me she is not leaving the house like that,* and *figuring out where the hell Noah is.*

Mom laughs from the balcony and reports, "He's tipping over every which way."

"Claudia will catch him," Noah mumbles.

"Claudia's catching him," Mom calls in.

I can just barely see Claudia and Gideon if I crane my neck and press my cheek around the window. Noah laughs because I look silly with my face all squished, but I like seeing my little siblings, pushing each other over, spinning in circles, always getting up. I can see Claudia's hands moving, but she's too far away for me to know what she's signing.

God, I can taste the ocean. I'm weak. "Let's go out, Noah."

He shakes his head and says, "We've got to wait for Melinda and the twins." This is so weird, because usually it's Noah trying to go somewhere—the movies, out for a run, college—and me begging him to stay, to wait, though I never have a specific thing for him to wait for.

"Noah, Chase, come sit with me," my father says. "You'll still be able to see the headlights, I promise."

This is enough of an excuse for me to abandon our stakeout. I give Noah a little head jerk, but he frowns and, instead of staying where he is, shows how disappointed he is by heavyfooting into the kitchen to put away groceries. He could not act more put-upon if it were his job. Whatever. I join my father on the couch and tuck myself under his arm while he strokes my hair.

I've just barely closed my eyes—the grain of the couch against my cheek, Noah's malcontented grumblings in my ear—when I see the headlight glare through the windows and through my eyelids.

"Noah, they're here!"

We run barefoot across the street to the Hathaways' and maul Melinda, Bella, and Shannon as soon as they step out of the SUV. Their parents laugh, pushing back their sweaty bangs, hauling duffel bags out of the car. Shannon pulls out of my hug and taps his fist against mine. He sticks his hand in my hair. "Welcome back, soldier," he says.

"Welcome home, Shannon."

"Can we make s'mores, Mom?" Bella asks. She's clinging to one of Noah's arms, which is kind of weird. I wrap the hem of Noah's shirt around my finger until I have a good enough hold to tug him away from her.

He's not even paying attention, because Melinda is milling by the other arm. She's nineteen, older than Noah, and so thin that she always looks like a part of her is missing and the rest of her might be about to go find it. Her long fingernails close the gap between her hand and Noah's wrist. I've seen Claudia do the same grip when she wants Noah to do something.

Melinda is his sister in a different way.

"Of course we can," Mrs. Hathaway says, with a laugh like a string instrument. "You boys want to get your family here?"

Noah says, "Chase, run and get everybody."

I sprint across the street and straight onto the beach. I'm in the sand for the first time this summer. I always forget how cold it feels on my feet. "Claude!"

Claudia's wearing her first two-piece bathing suit. She bought it around February, when they put the first bathing suits on the racks, and she's been clamoring to wear it ever since. I pretty much hate that some company thinks her pre-teen body is capable of being sexualized, and that this—this night, this beach—is the time and place to do it. She screams, "Chase!" and tackles me into the sand, and she's a child no matter what she's wearing.

"Melinda and the twins are here," I say. "Get dressed and we'll make s'mores."

But Claudia's already running across the street. "Gimme a shirt, Mom!" she yells, and Mom tosses down some old T-shirt of mine. Claudia doesn't stop running as she catches it and pulls it over her sweaty hair.

"Gid!" I yell. He's deaf as a board, but he's still spent all six years of his life getting yelled at. He's watching me, asking me with his eyes and his hands where Claudia went.

Across street I sign to him. **Come here. Don't fall down.** My ASL sucks, but the light's so bad right now it doesn't matter. Gideon runs over to me and I sign **hold my hand** before we start across the street. Either he sees this or just holds out of habit.

At the Hathaways', we make s'mores on the grill, pushing down on them with the spatula until they hiss. I sit with Shannon at the Hathaways' picnic table and we try to fill each other in on our lives since last August. During the year, I always feel like there are a million things I need to remember to tell him, and now nothing seems important but our siblings and our summer and the smoke from the grill.

Shannon keeps asking about my family—mostly Claudia and the baby yet to come—and I'm trying to pay attention, but my eyes keep going back to Bella. Was she this tall last summer? Maybe that's why she was hanging off of Noah. I'm still waiting to hit my growth spurt. But I'm the one who's her age. I hope she keeps that in mind.

I respond to one of Shannon's questions about Claudia with a quick, "I always forget how old she is," and then clear my throat. "So what's Bella been up to?"

Shannon looks over at his twin. She dances in circles in the spots of moonlight that break through the Hathaways' awning. Her bare feet glitter. They're white and pointed, like something off a fairy.

He smiles. "She got the lead in the *Nutcracker* this year." It's his turn to ask about someone. "So how's Gideon?"

Gideon's hugging on to Mom's leg, watching Claudia, probably wishing she were talking to him because she's the only one of us who signs well. The rest of us really only pretend we can, but, then again, so does Gideon.

"Deaf," I say. "Melinda?"

"Grumpy. And she dyes her hair a lot. She's always sighing and mumbling about the universe."

But right now Melinda's at the corner of the balcony, talking to the dogs. "Mom?" she says. "I'm taking the dogs out for a run."

Her mother is by the grill with my parents, where they're laughing over a few beers, throwing coals down to the sand, touching Mom's huge stomach.

Shannon says, "Chase? How's Noah?"

"I'll come with you," Noah says, with a glance Melinda's way, and he has the dogs unclipped from their leashes and free in no time, and he's gone, chasing them across the street and onto the beach. I listen for the sound of them splashing in the water, but they're too far away. I am getting a headache, listening this hard.

I try to think about Bella again, and I don't answer Shannon, but his father asks me the same question when I go over to the grill to collect my s'more. He claps me on the shoulder and says, "Noah excited for college?"

I want to tell him Noah doesn't really get excited, but I don't know how to describe my brother to someone who's known him just as long as I have but doesn't understand him any better. So I smile. It's so dark now, but the coals and the stars illuminate my siblings and Shannon's siblings and our parents and make us all look permanent and important.

I say, "He's kind of quiet about how he feels."

"Yeah. Did he run off with Melinda?"

"I guess so."

My parents exchange looks, like they were expecting Noah and Melinda's flighty romance to take a hiatus this year, or something.

Noah does not ruin tradition. I could have told them that. And Melinda is his summer. More and more every single year.

So I just say, "He runs off a lot."

Mr. Hathaway laughs and says, "Man, your brother's a flight risk, isn't he?" He serves me a s'more and says, "Still playing guitar, Chase?"

I grin and look down.

They drag their old guitar out so I don't have to run home, and I make up chord progressions while Bella sings along in this ghost voice that makes me hyperaware, like my whole body is made of fingertips. They smile at me in that way adults do when they're drunk that makes you feel not so much younger.

We carry the plates into the kitchen, where the lights dazzle us into submission until someone has the sense to dim them. Once all the dishes are cleaned and stacked, the adults convince us to run down to the beach and try to find Noah and Melinda.

He's up to his waist in the ocean, the Hathaways' two dogs swirling around him like they're trying to create a whirlpool. My brother is the eye of his manufactured hurricane.

"Get in!" he yells, and none of us needs to be told twice.

The six of us splash in after him, screaming at the cold water, screaming at each other, screaming at every single foot of empty where the sky is and we aren't. Bella's on my shoulders and I'm twirling her around, Melinda's holding her breath for as long as she can, everyone's always yelling, "Where's Gideon?" and pulling him out from underneath a breaking wave, yelling, "Where's Noah?" and realizing he's swum halfway out to sea.

Whenever there's a split second of silence, we can hear our parents across the street, strumming the old guitar, laughing, clinking their beer bottles together.

Eventually my brother the flight risk comes and holds my head underwater until everything swirls, and, when I come up and sputter and blink, everyone's skin is shiny and spotted from the stars. Bella and Claudia are running around on the sand, throwing handfuls at each other, shrieking, and Melinda's squeezing the ocean out of her somehow colorless hair, her legs absolutely sparkling.

I want to be exactly this old forever.

"Y'all right, soldier?" Shannon asks me, his voice raspy from the salt.

I nod and count heads. There's Claudia, Gideon, Melinda, Bella, Shannon . . . there's everyone but Noah, who somehow managed to disappear in that split second I wasn't watching him.

So I look at Shannon and smile, and I try not to care, I try not to worry that my brother will leave me for good, because nothing is as permanent or important as the first summer night. Bella's voice puts mine to shame, but I sing anyway, until Shannon dunks me underwater. When I come up, I hear everyone's laugh—Shannon's and Bella's, as identical as they aren't; Claudia's, trying to be a woman; Gideon's— that haunted sound that he doesn't know he's making—and Melinda's. Twinkling into Noah's ear as he swims back, back to her and not to me.

TWO

U p."

I'm sticking to the sheets with sweat, and the smell of Noah's sandals attacks my face. It is so summer.

At home, we each get our own rooms, but here, Noah and I share, even though there are enough rooms for us each to have our own. Part of the feeling of summer depends on waking up when he wakes up, or putting on a shirt gritty with sand and sunscreen that might not even be mine.

Claude and Gideon used to share too, but yesterday Claudia decided she wants her own room, since she's a woman now. Dad and I are both sure she's going to end up crashed on Gid's floor, listening to the weird noise he makes when he sleeps.

Noah's already dressed, rubbing sunscreen on his arms. His muscles wrap around him like extension cords. "Dad's making waffles," he says.

I sit up and rub my hair. It's pretty thin, like a baby's or something, and right now it feels like I have more sand in my scalp than hair.

Our family's divided in half between the blonds—Dad, Claudia, and me—and the brunets—Mom, Noah, and Gideon. The new baby will break the tie, provided she really is the last of the McGills. Our parents promised no more kids after this one. Which is good. I mean, I love my big family, but this is getting out of hand. I can barely name them all in one breath as it is.

I say, "How was your night?" because Noah didn't get to our room until late last night.

"Monumental."

"Yeah?"

"A very important night in the life of Noah, if I do say so myself."

"Okay, I want details. Graphic ones. Possibly pictures."

He makes a face. "Breakfast."

"You're not going to tell me?"

"Right now, I am telling you that it is time for breakfast, you lazy asshole. Get thee to a waffle."

Goddamn it. "All right, all right, I'm up."

Downstairs, Claudia is flipping through TV shows, all her hair combed out down her back. Claudia's the best blond of all of us. Her hair's the color of a banana—the fruit, not the peel.

Gideon's sitting at the table in his swim trunks and snorkel. **Awesome** I sign to him.

Thank you.

Noah rubs the top of Gideon's head on the way to the cabinet. Noah knows the least sign language of all of us, since he was already twelve when Gideon was born and past that time when your brain's willing to learn a new language. Claude, who was five, picked it up just like she picked up English. Mom is great—the motherly instinct outweighed the closed-brain thing—while Dad's about the same as I am. It's all a matter of how hard ASL was for us, and has nothing to do, sadly, with how much we want to talk to Gideon, in which case Mom and Dad would both be fluent and Noah and I would be fine just to smile.

Noah says, "Chase, ask Gid how he's going to eat waffles with a snorkel in his mouth."

I sign **eat how?**

Magic says Gideon.

"Magic," I repeat to Noah, and Dad laughs from the stove.

Noah gives Dad a stiff kiss on the cheek. "Where's Mom?"

Dad does that laugh that sounds like a cough. "Still fast asleep. I told her she needed to tuck in early last night, but she never listens to me. Looks like we'll be reheating some waffles for Mama, right, Claudia?"

Claudia looks up from the TV. "Is this because I'm a girl? I'm getting roped into reheating duties because I'm a *girl*?"

I let my mouth gape open. "*Girl?* I thought you were a *woman!*"

Noah laughs, and Claudia says, "Play your guitar, Chase."

I sit on the couch and start playing a blues tune for Claudia. "Poooor Claudia," I sing. "Drowning in brothers."

"New baby's a girl!" she cheers.

"With her luck it'll beeeee another brother!" I strum some final chords and everyone applauds, even Gideon.

Noah shovels down four waffles and gets very, very impatient waiting for the rest of us to finish. "I want to go downtown," he keeps whining, hanging off the counter, jostling Gideon's shoulder, trying to get us to hurry. **Out** he signs.

Waffles Gideon signs back, frowning.

"Claaaaude," Noah whines. "Chaaase."

"Shitdamn, Noah," I explode. Shitdamn is Dad's word, but sometimes it's too perfect to pass up. "Go outside and wear yourself out. We'll be ready in a minute."

Noah disappears for a few minutes and returns when we're rinsing the dishes in the sink. His pants are bunched by his ankles, gritty and slimy with sea foam and sand, and Gideon's blue plastic shovel is slung over his shoulders.

"Well?" we say.

Noah's panting. "I dug a really big hole."

Claudia wipes her hands on her shirt. "Gid'll fall in it." Gideon's messed-up ears mean sometimes he falls down just standing still.

"Gid needs to wear a helmet at all times."

We all turn and look at Gideon, who's standing in the center of the kitchen, spinning in circles, making gurgling noises through his snorkel.

"Ready to go?" Noah asks.

Time at the beach house is split between the ocean and downtown. Midday, we build sand castles, bury each other, play in the waves, and get sunburned, but mornings and nights are spent scouring the stores downtown and sweating sunscreen on the creaky playground. Noah used to play basketball, before he lost the ability to have what he calls "unproductive fun."

I wonder what digging that hole was, then. He probably didn't enjoy it, so it didn't count.

I say, "Maybe Bella can come?"

Claudia makes a face. "Bella's a snob."

"Shut up." She has some weird rivalry with Bella. Maybe she feels the same way about her as I do about Melinda, though I don't think Bella's ever stolen me away from my younger sibling. I wish.

"No girls," Noah says, and he tucks his arm around my shoulders and mumbles into my hair, "I'm tired." I look up, and he's giving me a significant look.

"Shitdamn," I mumble.

"Except me!" Claudia says. "I'm coming."

"Yes, yes." Noah palms Claudia's head. "You don't count."

"Because I'm a *woman.*"

"Sure."

"Unlike Bella and Melinda!"

Noah seems to give this more consideration than it deserves.

He drives us downtown. It's less than three miles, but Claudia still shouts up to the front seat every ten seconds that I need to change the radio station, and the trip still takes forever because Noah won't go even five miles over the speed limit. While we're shouting at each other, we sign variations of **seat belt** and **stay** and **no!** to Gideon, and I wonder if his escape-the-booster-seat persistence means he's going to grow up into a Noah.

Noah parallel parks, and we split up; he takes Claudia out to pick up stuff for my birthday dinner next week, and I bring Gid over to Recess, the toy store that's about five feet by five feet and *packed* with useless shit. I like to overstimulate Gideon sometimes. I feel like he doesn't get overwhelmed enough.

He gets sick of me latching on to him and uses his free hand to sign **hand no**.

Hand mine I sign back, and I keep a firm grip.

He cheers up when I show him posters of Marilyn Monroe and eventually convinces me to buy him a lunch box with her face on it. I can't believe I'm the one turning fifteen in a week, and I'm buying presents for him. **My birthday** I sign to him while I'm checking out. **You gift give me**.

Little brother me he says, spinning in circles, and the checker looks at us like we're crazy as he uses his hands for nothing but giving out change.

It's mid-July, so downtown is crawling with people. Girls in bikinis are walking with other girls in bikinis, their hair identically messed in those damp halfhearted buns, eye makeup smudging even though they think it's not. I like these girls, but they never smile back. The girls who smile back are always the ones who are wearing way too many clothes, the ones I want to throw in the ocean, or at the very least shake and say, "Do you know where you are?"

Gideon, who I have assigned to phone patrol, tugs my sleeve and points to his pocket. My cell phone is vibrating.

"Hello?"

"Can you stop at Candy Kitchen and get me some chocolate turtles?" Mom's voice reminds me of how she sounds at the beginnings of all her pregnancies when she throws up all the time and she calls Noah me or me Dad or Gideon Claudia—not that he notices.

I turn Gideon around so we're facing the direction we came from and almost get him killed by a boogie board–wielding preteen. Gideon crosses his arms and frowns at me.

Sorry I sign, hand against chest. To Mom, I say, "Didn't Dad say no more candy?"

"Dad can have say over candy rights when he's carrying the baby. And I swear to God, Chase, he's doing the next one."

"You promised no more babies."

She exhales. "Oh, you never know."

Watch. It's twins, and this is her way of breaking the news to me.

A Jeep pulls into the parking lot, teenagers clinging to its naked frame. They leap out before the car's even stopped, and their bodies *shuck* from sticking to the seats. I am so, so jealous. I can totally picture myself, two years from now, driving the shit out of one, or maybe next year or next week, sandwiched in the back with Shannon on one side and Bella on the other, my thigh sticking to hers, laughing and singing along with the radio, the pop songs I don't know during the year that I learn in just a few days here. . . .

Gideon tugs on me and says he wants to go back to the store. I shake my head.

I tell Mom, "Claude's just going to eat it all."

"Get Claude a bag of what she wants, and tell her she must stay away from the turtles on pain of death."

"I don't know what she wants. She's not with me." I'm sick of Gideon practically getting steamrolled by everyone on the sidewalk who assumes he can hear them approaching, so I scoop him up and put him on my back. His empty lunch box swings against my hip bone.

Mom says, "Where is Claudia?" in that voice that's supposed to be panicked, but when you have four kids—especially when those four kids are *us*—you have to get used to their disappearances, and Mom has.

"With Noah."

Gideon babbles in my ear as we head toward Candy Kitchen. It so, so freaks me out when he speaks. I turn around as much as I can and put my finger over my lips, but he ignores me.

"You left her with Noah?" Mom says.

Gideon sticks his hand in front of my face and fingerspells my name. God knows what he wants, but I sign **not now** over my shoulder the best I can, but he can't see the **not** underneath my chin, so he's freaking out trying to tell me whatever he thinks I just told him he could tell me. It's a good thing he somehow keeps a good grip, because between pidgin signing to him and trying not to drop Mom into the sno-ball–coated gutter, I have exactly no hands to make sure my little brother doesn't crack his head open on the pavement. His thighs are practically squeezing me in half.

Mom says, "You can't leave the kids with Noah!"

"I have Gideon."

My family's cure for Noah's irresponsibility is to pretend that I'm the oldest child.

"Claudia's *eleven*," I say. "She's not going to get kidnapped."

My mom says, "What was she wearing?"

Okay, so it's totally not my responsibility what Claudia wears. But she was dressed a little provocatively for anyone who's not twenty-one. And a whore.

I say, "Do you want me to go check the status of your daughter, or do you want me to get candy?"

After a pause, Mom says, "Candy."

Of course.

She says, "But I will not take it lightly if I only have three children left when you return!"

"Have a new one," I say, and I hang up. I set Gideon down and make him walk the rest of the way to Candy Kitchen. I want to complain about Mom, but I don't know the signs. Plus he's six years old and, more importantly, one of the brunets. Eventually, he's going to end up on Mom's side, and I want to keep him for as long as possible. Which means I can't let him know that there's a rift.

Snake he tells me, pointing to the toys at the corner of the store—particularly to a purple snake that could wrap around his neck and strangle him in his sleep.

No snake I sign back, while I choose a bag of chocolate turtles.

Now Gideon's playing with all the talking dolls, squeezing their hands so they talk at different times, their hollow voices overlapping while they echo one another, like a badly synchronized Gregorian chant. I close my eyes as I dig money out of my pocket and try to pretend everyone isn't staring at him. Staring at me, asking me to *do something.*

"Gideon," I say. He obviously ignores me and keeps

squeezing their hands. Everyone's still looking at me, so I say, "Okay, I'm sorry my deaf brother has no sense of rhythm."

They look away like they suddenly noticed he's disfigured.

I give him Mom's turtles to put in his lunch box, which shuts him up for a little while. He shakes it all the way to the little grocery store and feels the chocolate moving around in there. **Eat** he signs to me.

No no no. Mom.

Mom hate he says, and opens his lunch box to look at the turtles.

Lie, but he's not looking at me.

I lead Gideon into the tiny grocery store. Noah's by one of the registers, scanning the magazines. "You're not supposed to be here!" Noah says, hiding something behind his back, but I'm too busy being stunned that Noah's where he's supposed to be. "I could be buying you a present right now," he says.

"That's totally porn behind your back."

"Yeah, but it could be a birthday card. You don't know my life."

"I'm looking for Claudia."

Mom hate Mom hate Mom hate Gideon's signing. Noah puts his finger over his lips. I know he's telling Gid to be quiet, but the gesture's uncomfortably close to the sign for **true.**

I say, "Where's Claudia?"

"Oh." He looks over his shoulder. "Uh, she's around here somewhere—"

"Noah!" I prowl the whole grocery store, scanning up and down each of its ten aisles. I see a dozen girls who look like Claudia, but no Claudia.

He waves his hand. "She's fine."

"Who the hell even knows where she is. . . ."

"This isn't exactly *Claudia Does Manhattan*. There are, like, twenty stores here."

"The streets are *mobbed*." I grab Gideon's wrist so he'll shut up. "She could be *anywhere*."

"Chase, she's not a baby. She'll be fine. Now get out of here. I'm trying to get you a nice card, okay? And it's creepy to look at naked girls with Gid here."

All the people on the streets, at the basketball courts, in the Jeeps, and pouring in and out of the burger place suddenly look more sinister. Because none of them are my baby sister.

Claudia I sign to Gideon.

Beach dig go want he signs, jumping from foot to foot.

No. Claudia where?

Dig big big Noah same.

No, no, not Noah. Don't be like Noah. I keep a firm grip on his wrist and pull him toward the playground. **Dizzy** he complains.

The innocent little girls on the swing set are not my sister. They look about fifteen years too young. If people act like I'm older than Noah, I've always felt, somehow, that Claudia's older than me. At least during the summers. It's probably because Shannon's had a crush on her practically since she was born, or because during the year she goes back to being my baby sister, and during the summer she's a cat in heat. And it's worse every single year, just like Noah's whatever with Melinda.

Where is she?

Scared Gideon signs, and points at me.

Am I scared?

I sign **dead sister don't want** which is really cruel of me, but at least it gets Gideon to shut up.

I wait for a family devouring frozen yogurt to clear the nearest bench so Gid and I can sit down. He crawls the length of the bench, getting sandy yogurt residue all over his fingers and his hand-me-down clothes.

Okay. If I were Claudia, I would be . . .

The only logical ending I can figure for the sentence is: using that genius I.Q. to find a new, functional family.

Find! Gideon says.

What?

He points, and there's Claudia. Of course—the other ending for that sentence. If I were Claudia, I would be . . . hanging into some stranger's car.

"Claudia!"

She turns to me, laughter frozen in her smile, and rolls her eyes at me. "Hold on," I see her say into the car. "It's my boyfriend."

"Stop it." I yank her away from the window and pull her toward the grocery store. "You're eleven. *Eleven*. I am not your boyfriend."

"Aw, Chase." She pulls Gideon up and carries him like a baby, then sees his lunch box and laughs. "You think your siblings are growing up too fast, Chasey? Who's buying his brother a Marilyn Monroe lunch box?"

"Yeah, because he's really going to jerk off to a lunch box. Don't translate that!" Claudia has this habit of signing to Gideon everything we say in front of him, which is a problem when we are saying things, as we usually are, that Gideon doesn't need to hear.

"We can't stay infants forever, Chase." Claudia tosses her hair over her shoulder. "It's summer! It's hot! Things are happening! Let things happen, darling!"

It is becoming such a struggle not to roll my eyes whenever Claudia talks.

"I found her," I tell Noah, pushing her in front of him. "Look. Alive. Thank me."

Noah shakes his head at Claudia, and for a second I think he's going to scold her. "He needs to *relax*," he quips to her.

"I know, right?" She sets Gideon on the ground. "He holds on like *crazy*."

Noah sees I'm still pissed off when we get back in the car, so he tunes the radio to one of my favorite summer songs—grungy, sticky rock that makes my mouth taste like sunscreen—and Claudia, for once, doesn't ask to change the station, and just busies herself with keeping Gideon in his car seat.

"Trying to hold on to him, are you?" I call back, but she pretends she can't hear me. She makes a silly face at me the next time I look back. She's still on the blond team, no matter what, no matter that a lot of the time I'd rather have Noah and leave Claudia out for the seagulls.

THREE

S hannon has smears of black sand under his eyes and a big pointy stick in his right hand. "The warrior approaches prey," he whispers.

I'm on my belly in the sand beside him, scraping the beginnings of my sunburn. "Prey continues to be completely unaware of its fate."

Yawning, Melinda flips a page in her magazine and reaches underneath the rim of her sunglasses to scratch her eye.

"The prey is one hundred percent in sight," Shannon says, taking a silent step forward. Already, the sock tan around his ankles is starting to fade. "On the signal, the warriors will strike."

"One," I whisper, and I hitch my feet up to scootch closer. Melinda crosses her legs and her beach chair squeaks.

"Two," breathes Shannon.

"Three!"

We rush at Melinda and grab the back of her chair. She shrieks, and all three of us go down in a heap of sand and sweat and swimsuits. The attack's over, but Melinda's still screaming, kicking, hitting us with her magazine.

"You boys are awful!" she squeaks, picking herself up off the ground.

Shannon and I are laughing too hard to move.

"Fifteen!" she says. "You're fifteen!"

"I'm still fourteen," I choke.

"Yeah, you're Chase Everboy McGill."

"What?"

"Always and forever a boy."

She tries, worthlessly, to dust herself off, then gives up and heads toward the ocean. I try very hard not to watch her ass, to remember that she's Noah's, even though Noah went missing hours ago.

"You two *are* completely mental." Bella's hand wraps around my arm, and she pulls me and Shannon to our feet.

"You better go rinse off or that sand's going to be stuck to you forever."

"You coming?" Shannon asks.

"Nuh-uh. I'm working on my tan." Bella smiles—she has a Melinda smile-in-training—and heads back over to where our parents are spread out with their coolers and towels and umbrella. She looks over her shoulder when she's almost there, meets my eyes, and bites her lip.

I'm so jealous, instantly. I want to bite her lip.

Shannon claps me on the shoulder. "Once you marry Bella and I marry Claudia, soldier, we will have it made."

I look at him incredulously. *"Dude."*

He laughs. "I know, I know. We already have it made."

It's about two o'clock on Wednesday and the sun's at its hottest and yellowest, all prepared to fry our skin into that perfect almost-August brown. It's the kind of hot where every step feels like it should be rewarded with applause.

Claudia and Gideon have built this huge castle. It's almost, but not quite, too far up the beach for the waves to crawl, and they're screaming and rebuilding while it gets slowly destroyed. Or Claudia is, at least; Gideon's just screaming constantly.

"You should get him hearing aids," Shannon tells me, as we start wading in.

"Wouldn't do any good." I squidge my toes into the wet sand. "They only work if you have some base hearing. Gid has nothing."

"But then everyone would know he's deaf. They'd stop staring." I follow his gaze and look around the beach. It's crowded, but there's enough room for us all to pretend that we're the only ones here—until one family's six-year-old makes an inordinate amount of noise, I guess. Chubby mothers with orange peroxided hair and fathers with Bud Light and children who are so happy and adorable they don't even seem real are all either looking at my brother or over at our parents, trying to figure out who is responsible for him.

I would honestly go to each and every one of these people and calmly explain that trying to be responsible for Gideon is like trying to be responsible for Noah, if that would mean anything to them, or if the idea of relating Gideon to Noah *again* didn't make my stomach toss.

"You watching him?" I ask Claudia.

She rolls her eyes, digging with a tiny blue shovel. "Of course."

"Don't let him get dizzy."

"He's always dizzy." Claudia throws a hunk of sand Gideon's way to get his attention, but it gets in his eyes and he shrieks.

"Claude . . ." I splash out of the water and wipe Gideon's face off with the edge of my bathing suit. **Cry no** I tell him.

He throws sand at me.

I sign **dizzy?**

He signs **blue** and flops down in the sand. Blue? What the hell? And I *just* wiped his eyes off, for God's sake. He has to go and take a pile of sand to the face?

Shannon says, "Chase, c'mon!"

"Coming." I'm not going to spend the whole day baby-sitting.

I go back into the water where Shannon's floating on his back and Claudia's collecting water in her pail. "Keep an eye on him," I tell her. I'm always afraid Gideon will wander in the water, get dizzy, and forget which way's back to shore.

She says, "There is a lifeguard, you know."

"Only until six."

"Yeah. It's two."

"I know . . ."

"Chase." She squeezes my hand. "I'm watching him, okay?"

"Okay." Good. That's it. I'm done worrying. I'm not supposed to be the one looking after all of us. This isn't supposed to be my clan.

I swim out to Shannon, and he pulls his head out of the

water to look at me. Like he can read my mind—and would that really surprise me after this long?—he says, "Where's Noah?"

"I don't know." I pulse my legs like a jellyfish. "I never know."

"I guess him splitting all the time means you won't miss him too bad when he goes to college, yeah?"

No, him splitting all the time means I've missed him for as long as I can remember. I sink underneath the water and open my mouth. I taste all the salt and the microscopic creatures.

Once I'm out of the water and finished drying out my ears, I flop down in the sand next to my father. He's tearing through his battered copy of *Twenty Thousand Leagues Under the Sea*, sunglasses tucked into his blond hair.

"Hi," I say.

He sets down the book. "That was the most morose 'hi' I've ever heard in my life."

"I want Noah to be back for my birthday."

"That's nearly a week, Chase. I'm sure he'll be back by then."

We're leaving right after my birthday this year, which sucks. Normally we stay at least a week after. "This summer's too short."

"You don't want your new sister to be born on the beach, do you?"

I look at Mom, practically bursting through her maternity swimsuit, chatting with Mr. and Mrs. Hathaway, sipping a Diet Coke. By the ocean, Shannon's holding Gid by his waist, twirling him around, and Claudia's crying, "He'll get dizzy! He'll get dizzy!"

I kind of can't think of a better place for her to be born than right here on the beach, but I know that's stupid of me. I know babies need hospitals, but right now I can't imagine anyone needing anything more than this.

Dad kisses the top of my head. "Where do you think Noah goes?"

"Anywhere. He sits in bookstores or sleeps on people's couches or something. He doesn't care where he goes. I get that part."

"You get that part?"

I nod, tracing my initials in the sand.

"Which part don't you get, Chase?"

I clear my throat. "Why he goes."

When I wake up in the middle of the night, two days later, I first think it's because I forgot to close Noah's window, and it's chilly. Then I hear *clip . . . clip . . . clip* like tiny, slow-motion horses.

"*Chase.*"

I crawl over to Noah's bed and kneel on his unmussed covers. I lean out the window and there he is, up to his ankles in the sand beside our house.

"Let me in, man," he says, in that quiet voice that's so low it sounds loud.

"Noah, it's three in the morning."

He smiles, and it's like his mouth is producing its own light. "That's why I'm throwing rocks at your window, dumbass, and not Mom and Dad's."

It's your window, dumbass.

"Dad's sleeping on the couch," I say. "He'll hear you come in."

"They fought?"

"Yeah." They fight so much that these are usually the only ones we worry about now: the fights that last long enough for them to sleep in different places.

"Shit." Noah exhales slowly, then shrugs. "Oh, well. Maybe he'll be happy I'm home."

Dad is not happy he's home. He's rarely happy about anything when Mom's exiled him, but he's really, really pissed when Noah wakes him up sneaking through the front door. "Noah," he says. "*Noah.* Where were you?"

Noah shrugs, his hands in his pockets. "Just walking on

the beach. I visited the Hathaways. Got some pizza. Went down to Dewey—"

"You've been gone for . . . do you know what time it is?"

Noah groans and goes to the kitchen for a soda. "God. I'm eighteen, Dad."

"It has nothing to do with—"

"No, it has *everything* to do with that, man! I'm eighteen and I don't smoke and I don't drink and I don't do goddamn drugs, and if I want to get away for a little while, just let me do it!" He shakes his head, goes upstairs. *"Jesus."*

"Shitdamn." Dad lies down and fusses angrily with his quilt. "I don't even *know* what to *do* about that *boy*—"

"Brunets," I say, and shrug.

Dad looks up at me. "What is it? Does he just hate us?"

I don't know if he means us as a family or just him and Mom, but I shake my head.

"Then what is it?"

I don't know.

Upstairs, I repeat Dad's question in my voice. "What is it?" I ask Noah, sitting on my bed while he changes out of his sticky clothes. I'm still cold, but I'm sweaty now, and I'm feeling every grain of sand I tracked between my sheets.

He says, "There's no *it*, Chase. I just need to get out of

here sometimes. This combination of drama and no drama, it kills me sometimes, man. It's the silence and the not silence, do you get it? We make all this noise when there doesn't need to be noise and then when our father's sleeping on the couch, when there's an actual problem—do you hear that?"

I don't hear anything, but I'm used to not understanding a thing Noah says.

We're quiet for a minute, staring at the dark. Half my brain is asking the other half why I'm awake, and I can't think of a good answer.

Noah's cooling himself down. He walks in tight circles, takes small sips from his water bottle, pauses to mutter something to himself. He's gotten better at self-regulating lately, according to Mom. Eventually, he gives one last head shake and turns off the lights. I hear him crawling between his sheets and I crawl between mine.

We're quiet. When we were younger, these used to be the only times we really talked—here, with the lights off, allegedly falling asleep. We'd never know when a conversation was really over. We'd say, "Okay, that's enough, I'm so tired," but then one of us would burst out laughing thinking of something that happened earlier that day, and then we'd both be cracking up and sharing inside jokes and confessing things we never would in daytime and never sleeping. We don't do it as much anymore, but I think it's because we talk more in our everyday life now than we used to. We don't need to pretend that we only notice each other in the dark.

But I don't think we're done talking tonight.

He takes a slow breath and says, "Man, Mom's about to pop, isn't she?"

"Then you'll have two girls and two boys. How do you feel about that, Noah?"

He laughs, and I swear I hear him rolling his eyes. "I'll start building my ark. Chase?"

"Yeah?"

"Listen, I'm really not going anywhere interesting. Ever. But . . . you can come, okay?"

"I don't want to come." I roll onto my back. "I want you to be here. Sometimes. When we need you."

Quiet, then Noah laughs. "They should have named you Stay."

"That's an ugly-ass name."

He kicks his feet through the sheets. "Yeah, you're right."

FOUR

S he's eleven!" Noah and I protest the entire time Melinda's patting our sister's face with powder and dabbing lip gloss on her baby mouth. "Too young for makeup," I whine, and Noah drops his head onto Bella's pillow so he can't watch. But I can't look away. Bella and I are riveted— Bella by how old Claudia looks, me by the length of Melinda's fingers.

"I'm only giving her a little, Chasey." Melinda traces powder over the tops of Claudia's eyes. "Making her feel just as beautiful as she is."

Claudia's positively beaming.

"She's going to be swarmed," Noah says, his voice muffled. "Do you want her swarmed by *men?*"

Claudia laughs, all grown-up in the back of her throat. *Ha ha ha.*

"Maybe someone will fall in love with her," Bella says, and bites her lip and looks at me.

Noah looks at me, telling me it's my turn to object. "Too young to be someone's lust object," I say, then turn to Bella and mouth *Eleven,* to clarify. Bella had her makeup done before we got here, and now she's studying herself in the mirror, pinching her cheekbones and pressing the skin between her eyebrows.

"You're all too young to be talking about this love and lust shit," Noah says.

Melinda is calm, blowing extra eye shadow off her fingers. "The point is not to be loved. The point is to love." She puts on some kind of accent. "'*For there is merely bad luck in not being loved; there is misfortune in not loving.*'"

Noah picks up his head. "What's that?"

"Camus, darling." Melinda takes a book from the foot of her bunk and tosses it down to Noah. "Only the most summer-oriented philosopher in the book."

"What book?" says Bella.

Melinda examines her eyeliner pencil. "The book of life, my dear."

"Man," Claudia says. "That's one big book."

"Small font, too." Noah sits up and cracks open the paperback. "He's French?"

"*Oui*, but that's supposed to be the best translation." Melinda gathers her curly hair back in one hand and leans forward, examining Claudia's eyebrows. "You guys would like him."

Noah reads, "*'Turbulent childhood, adolescent daydreams in the drone of the bus's motor, mornings, unspoiled girls, beaches, young muscles always at the peak of their effort, evening's slight anxiety in a sixteen-year-old heart, lust for life, fame, and ever the same sky through the years, unfailing in strength and light, itself insatiable, consuming one by one over a period of months the victims stretched out in the form of crosses on the beach at the deathlike hour of noon.'*"

We're quiet.

"Well." Claudia flinches at the mascara wand. "That was happy."

"Shut up," Noah says. "I'd almost believe he grew up here."

I look at him, and I know by the way he's smiling that I'm making the same face I always make when we agree. The one that looks really shocked.

"I think it's beautiful," Bella says, quietly.

"*No love without a little innocence,*" Melinda recites, putting on that silly accent again.

Noah says, "Hmm," and sticks the paperback in his pocket. "All right. You kids ready to go?"

The Jolly Roger isn't much of an amusement park, and it's farther away than we'll usually stand to travel when we're down here, but every few years we all get it in our heads that we need to go. We grab Shannon and Gideon from the living room, stuff ourselves into the van, and we're off to see the creaky fun house and the carousel and the clumsy juggler.

All the windows are down and the wind sounds like someone yelling at us, but we're laughing so hard we barely hear it. The girls rake their fingers through their hair to keep the tangles out, but it's hopeless and they know it and it's okay. The lights on every restaurant, mini-golf-course, ice-cream stand, and motel rush by just like the people, who are all dressed ten times better than they ever are during the year and trying ten times less hard. I feel like we're stuck in a movie reel, roaring through as hard as we can and spinning the world into streaks.

"*Gods of summer they were at twenty,*" Melinda says.

It takes Noah a few minutes to find this quote in his book.

"'*Gods of summer they were at twenty by their enthusiasm for life, and they still are, deprived of all hope. I have seen two of them die. They were full of horror, but silent.*'"

Melinda takes her eyes off the road to examine us all in the rearview mirror. Claudia, for a minute, stops punching Gideon and looks at us, her artificially enlarged eyes artificially sparkling. She's beautiful—just normal, unscary beautiful—without all the makeup, but she never carries herself like she is.

"Which two?" Claudia asks.

Noah's glued back to the book. "It could be an exaggeration."

"I need to get a copy of this book," I say.

Noah nods. "You so do, Chase. And so do I. . . ."

"What's mine is yours," Melinda says softly. "As long as I eventually get it back."

We park and wait by the ticket booths, calculating how much money we have and how many rides we need to go on. I'm trying to track everyone with my eyes; I feel older than the twins but younger than Claudia, who's standing with Melinda, tossing her matted hair, while Bella and Shannon shriek and climb on each other's backs. Gideon falls down. "Everyone needs tickets," I say. "Someone has to watch—"

"I've got it." Noah gives me one of those rare, reassuring

smiles. "Melinda and I will take Gideon, okay? And you stay with Claude and the twins."

I yank Gideon off the ground and sign **Noah stay.**

Noah run Gideon says, and I try not to concentrate on that.

Stay me? Noah signs.

I realize that we never try to do anything to Gideon without asking his permission. Even though he's six, and I don't think considering a six-year-old's opinion usually comes with the territory. Some parts of being deaf are pretty sweet, I guess.

Gid spins around for a little while, then falls down again and signs **OK.**

"C'mere, you." Noah hauls Gideon onto his back and smiles at Melinda. "We've got him."

This finally hits me. "Yeah, and what are you going to do with Gideon while you're with Melinda?"

"Cover his eyes."

"Oh, ha ha," I call to their backs.

Claudia and Shannon want to ride the log flume, so we walk across the park, crunching the gravel beneath our sandals. Every few steps Bella will look at me and smile. Whenever a girl from school is nice to me like this, I'm always tripping over myself figuring out how far I'm going to try to get with her and freezing up before I can do anything. But here, I have this feeling that I can't screw this up, and there's no point in planning anything, because what's going to happen is going to happen. It's as predictable as the carousel.

She doesn't want to get splashed, so we stand under the pavilion while Shannon and Claude get in line. Bella's wearing a pink skirt, and the breeze sometimes hitches it above her knees. Her legs are starting to tan, or maybe it's that brown lotion girls use to pretend. Either way, I like it even more than I would have expected.

"Really nice night, isn't it?" she says.

"Mmm-hmm."

She revolves, looking at the lights from the Ferris wheel bouncing off the water for the paddleboats. "I love it here."

"I love everywhere here." I rub the back of my neck. "I seriously wish we could live here, even in the off-season. Like, even when it's cold, this has got to be good."

"We come down in the fall and winter sometimes. I almost like it better. No people around, everything so gray . . . It feels really old. Like you're looking at this town a hundred years ago."

"When our forefathers ran around barefoot."

She smiles at me. "Exactly."

There's no one else under the pavilion, and with the

amusement park bouncing off Bella's eyes and the dusty pink of her skirt, I can almost pretend we are a hundred years old and we know everything. When, really, the only thing I know is that I'm going to kiss her, but I'm not going to try anything more. And she's smiling because she knows it too.

It's not really that we're old so much as we've existed forever. We're in a black-and-white photo. The only color comes from the Ferris wheel lights and her skirt.

We're eternalized in the film. Forever kids. We are our forefathers today.

I kiss her, and her mouth tastes like wax and peppermint.

It's not my first kiss, but it *feels* like it. Like I'm watching a movie of my first.

She pulls back, laughing. "Chase, you bit my lip."

Or a blooper reel. "I did? Sorry."

She giggles and turns, and I smell the powder on her cheek. I want to kiss her. I want to bake cookies with her. I want to watch her put on her makeup like I got to watch Claudia.

"Look." She points to the top of the flume. "They're going down."

"Shannon looks *terrified*."

"He's just hoping Claudia will hold his hand."

We watch Claudia and Shannon take the plunge, and I wrap my fingers around Bella's palm.

"Chase."

I look up from Camus. "Shh shh shh." I jerk my head to Noah, crashed on top of his covers, shoes still on. "He's asleep. And still, for once." Noah's always waking me up by thrashing around when he's sleeping. It's the worst.

Claudia tilts from one foot to the other, doing the same little dance that Gideon does. I close the paperback and say, "You're supposed to be asleep, beautiful."

"Mom and Dad are fighting."

"Come on. Don't let that worry you."

"I couldn't sleep."

I scoot over on my bed and she sits down, her nightgown pooling around her knees. She's washed all the makeup off and she got sunburned today, so she looks like my little sister again. It's something about winters and nighttimes that makes me remember how young Claudia is. It's when she's quiet. Her voice is old; she's always confused for our mother on the phone.

"Is this Camus stuff really any good?" she asks.

"He definitely knew his summers." I flip to one of my dog-eared pages. "'*Sometimes at night I would sleep open-eyed*

49

underneath a sky dripping with stars. I was alive then.'"

She stares at me. "You can't sleep with your eyes open."

"You are so literal, Claude. Come on. Remember . . . you've got to remember. When Gid was still a baby, and Dad used to take me, you, and Noah and set us up on deck chairs on the balcony at night? Wrap us all up in sleeping bags and tell us stories? And we'd hear the waves come in and it would always be too bright to sleep—"

"Because of the stars?"

"Well, because Mom had all the lights on inside, walking Gideon up and down the hall so he'd shut up, but . . . yeah. The stars, too."

Claudia sticks her head out my window. "I mean, I don't know if they're *dripping* exactly."

"The sky's dripping."

She doesn't speak for a minute, then says, "Oh."

I tuck her under my arm and hold her for a while. She says, "I don't really remember."

"Well. You were young."

"Don't remember before Gideon." She smiles. "Was I alive then?"

"I assure you that you were."

"Your birthday's in two days."

"Oh, really? I didn't know."

She sticks out her tongue.

"Go back to bed," I say. "Gideon will feel you walking around and get all upset." Gid can tell the vibrations of our footsteps apart, and if he wakes up and realizes Claudia isn't in bed where she's supposed to be he is going to freak out. He hates when he wakes up and people aren't where they're supposed to be. Before he goes to bed every night, he takes an inventory of where we are, and if we drift, we have to be so quiet.

She kisses my cheek. "Night, Chase."

"Night."

"'*No love without a little innocence,*'" Noah says, completely still.

"I thought you were asleep. You're so creepy."

He shrugs. "So how was your lovely innocent night?"

"I kissed her."

"What a man." But he says it warmly. "How was it?"

My first thought is to relate it to soft-serve ice cream, but I can already hear Noah laughing at that. "It was nice."

"God. God, really, it was nice?" He sounds so earnest that I think for a minute that he's making fun of me. He props himself up on an elbow. "God, I fucking miss when kisses were nice. I'm so jealous of people young enough to still have nice kisses."

"Wait, kissing isn't nice anymore?"

"No. It's foreplay. Trust me, you get old enough, and everything is foreplay. Kissing is foreplay. Talking is foreplay. Holding hands is foreplay. I swear to God, Chase, I think at this point, sex would be foreplay."

This would probably be a good time to ask if he and Melinda have really slept together, but I can't make myself say the words. So I just say, "That doesn't even make sense."

"Sex is a to-do list where nothing gets crossed out."

I find the passage Melinda quoted in my Camus book. *"'No love without a little innocence. Where was the innocence? Empires were tumbling down; nations and men were tearing at one another's throats; our hands were soiled. Originally innocent without knowing it, we were now guilty without meaning to be: the mystery was increasing our knowledge. This is why, O mockery, we were concerned with morality. Weak and disabled, I was dreaming of virtue!'"*

Noah looks at me and coughs, his eyebrows up in his bangs.

"What?" I say.

With a straight face, he recites, *"'I may not have been sure about what really did interest me, but I was absolutely sure about what didn't.'"*

"Come on. It's *foreplay?* Seriously?"

"You're too young." He flops backward. "You wouldn't understand. You are a fetus in a world of Camus and spermicidal lubricant."

"And you're an asshole."

"I'm just cynical. And you have no idea how far that's going to take me."

"Neither do you."

"Au contraire, little brother. I know exactly how this college game works. I will arrive, the dark horse in a band of mushy-hearted freshman. College will pee itself in terror of my disenfranchised soul."

I roll my eyes. "Beautiful."

"Look. Listen to my words of wisdom. College's only role these days, for an upper-middle-class kid going in for a fucking liberal arts degree, is very simple. Do you know what that is?"

"A diploma. A good job. Yay."

"No. College exists only because it thrives on the hopes and dreams of the young and innocent. College is a hungry zombie here to eat your brains. It wants to remind you that your naivete is impermanent and someday, English major or no, you'll wear a suit and hate the feeling of sand between your toes."

It's not going to happen to me.

Noah continues, in a low mutter, "Like that's not already

forced into our heads every single fucking minute of every winter."

"So you're, like, essentially already educated, just because you're an asshole?"

"Because I've resigned myself to my fate, yeah. I've pre-colleged myself. I'm rocking the institution, entering it already all disillusioned and shit. I'm going to single-handedly change the world of higher education."

I clear my throat. *"'I may not have been sure about what really did interest me, but I was absolutely sure about what didn't.'"*

"Go to sleep. Asshole."

I never have a hard time falling asleep, but I do tonight. It takes a while of thinking of Bella's lips before I drift off.

FIVE

I'm playing with a yo-yo under our house, sitting on one of the stilts that holds the foundation off the sand. All the houses here are raised at least eight feet off the ground. Otherwise they would wash away in a storm. A few years ago, I got tall enough to hoist myself up here and perch.

My eyes are focused on the Hathaways' house. I feel like you're supposed to see a girl after you kiss her. My father always said that girls will take any excuse to feel ignored. I don't want to go down that road. It would ruin everything.

When I see the front door to their house open, finally,

I let the yo-yo sleep. It's Bella, but she's with her mom.

They're screaming at each other—something about spending time with the family and paying too much for shoes.

There's so much about girls I don't understand. I don't know how I'm old enough to kiss them but not old enough to talk to them.

Whatever it means, in the grand scheme, right now it means that I don't talk to Bella for a while. I guess I'm a little scared.

Cake.

I sign **tomorrow**, not that time means anything to a six-year-old.

Cake now.

Birthday tomorrow.

I try to distract Gideon with the sunset over the ocean, but he's not having any of that. Then Shannon and Noah run past with the dogs at their heels, and his hands scream at me to let him down so he can chase them.

"Be careful!" I yell after him.

From behind me, Melinda laughs. "All these years and you still shout at him."

I turn around and watch her walk toward me, her long arms swinging against the hem of her skirt. I look away. My siblings and her siblings are all running around barefoot together. "Habit, I guess. I have two other siblings to yell at."

"And number three on her way. You excited?"

"Yeah, totally. Hoping it'll . . ." I drift off, my eyes following Bella as she collects seashells down by the shore.

"Was there a sentence to be completed there?"

I smile. "Put us back together. I'm hoping it'll put us back together."

She puts her hand in my hair. "Something got you down, Chasey?"

"I was just telling Claudia about how stuff used to be, and it's just so . . . *used* to be."

She nods and slips her hand back into the kangaroo pocket of her hoodie. "Noah used to be around more." But she's not with Noah now, even though he's here. She's standing here with me, and I don't know why.

I say, "Noah used to be around a lot more. But that feels forever ago." I rub my hair. It's dry as dust. "Before we knew that Gid was deaf, I guess. Made stuff get complicated."

She says, "You guys do okay, though. I mean, he's happy. Playing with Bella and Shannon."

"He can't talk to them. We can barely talk to him."

"What's the point of talking?"

"We're talking right now."

"But we're not saying anything."

There's a particularly loud wave, and I watch them all stay on their feet before I breathe. I wish Noah would get the dogs farther away from the water, so I could relax for a minute, enjoy the smell of Melinda's perfume.

"What you just said," I say. "Was that Camus?"

"No, silly." Her fingernails stroke my cheek, and then her lips press onto their tracks. "That was Hathaway," she whispers.

After the kids are asleep, I'm making tea for Mom, alone in the kitchen, when Noah comes up behind me and claps his hands on my shoulders. "Want to give you your birthday present," he tells me, giving each arm a squeeze before he lets go.

"Don't do that."

"All right. I can just return it. Free money!"

"It's not my birthday."

He scratches his nose and peers at the tea kettle. "Tomorrow."

"So give it to me tomorrow. Please?" I hate, hate, hate begging Noah. "Please. Please give it to me tomorrow."

He crosses his arms. "Chase, come on. I just . . . might not be around tomorrow."

"Please. Be around. Can that be my birthday present, Noah, please? Can you be around?"

"Happy birthday to you," he sings, softly, opening some weird cabinet that we never use underneath the sink.

"Noah."

"Happy birthday to you."

"Noah!"

"Happy birthday, dear Chasey," he whisper-sings, and hands me a small, horribly wrapped package.

It takes me a second to figure out what it is—some long piece of embroidered canvas—and then it hits me like a brother in a wrestling match. It's a guitar strap.

"You made this."

Noah wrings his hands in that way. "Yeah, returning it would have been kind of a bitch."

I spread the strap out on the counter and look at it. It's divided into five colors—blue, then yellow, then red, purple, and green, and each is stitched with names. Noah, then Chase, then Claudia, Gideon, and Newbaby.

"She'll have a real name soon," I say.

Noah shrugs. "She'll always be Newbaby."

I pick my guitar up off the ground and detach the old, ugly strap. "Noah, this is amazing."

He shrugs. "Thought you'd like it."

"Love it." Love him. I strum a few chords. "Noah. Please, please be here tomorrow?"

He rolls his eyes. "You stupid boy," he says, and touches the strap by my shoulder, where his name is. "I'm always here."

There's so much I want to say—*Don't give me clichés when I need a brother, don't act like you can't hear me when I know you can, give me a hug, give me an answer, give me a song title,* but he's rescuing the whistling teapot and bringing a mug out to Mom. I lean against the counter and play, singing to myself. I don't know how I ended up with three, almost four, siblings and no one to sing backup.

SIX

S treamers," Claudia says decisively, and she starts taping from one corner of the kitchen to the other. "If dinner's going to be cold, we must at least have streamers."

Cake Gideon signs, with a hard nod.

"Do whatever." I fingerpick. "Claudia, tell him *do whatever*. I don't know how to sign that."

Claudia slaps the backs of her fingers against each other, and Gideon falls down.

It's almost nine o'clock and we still haven't eaten, still haven't sung "Happy Birthday," still haven't cut a slice of cake for Gideon. Because Noah is gone, and Mom and Dad can't decide if we should start our family party without him.

"He's our *son*," Mom says. They're arguing upstairs, with their door shut, and we can still hear them.

"He's *never here*."

I feel like every family's supposed to have a rebel, but right now I care less about what we're supposed to do and what Noah's supposed to do and more that my little brother's wanted cake for two days and it's sitting melting on the countertop. He can see it. I can see it. Can we give my brother some cake?

"Don't worry about them," Claudia says, scissors between her teeth, nodding upstairs toward our parents. "Everything will be fine."

Gideon's dancing.

"I wanted Noah to be here." I put down my guitar and start picking up the place settings. "I told him. I said, '*Noah, can you please be here?*'"

"Yeah, and you thought he'd change for you?"

Maybe. "I thought he'd listen to me."

"Yeah, because listening is really Noah's forte." She signs to Gideon, too quickly for me to see, and he runs upstairs.

I say, "I'm the only one he ever listens to. When he listens. And I don't appreciate it when you send Gideon into war zones."

62

"He's just going to try to hurry them along."

I flop down in a kitchen chair. "He's not a tool, Claude."

"He is, actually. A really good one." She rolls her eyes. "I'm just kidding, but, come on. He'll walk in there and spin around and do that smile, and Mom and Dad will make some final snotty remarks at each other and stop fighting, and we can have your birthday. Isn't that what you want?"

"No. I want *Noah*."

We have one set of good plates at the beach house, and Mom set them out. It makes putting them away harder.

"So he leaves sometimes," Claudia says. "So he's not the nicest guy in the world. Get over it, Chase. Everyone else has."

"Not Dad."

"If he is in this family, he cannot just keep leaving!" Dad shouts from upstairs.

"Yeah, keep on being just like Dad." Claudia's eyes keep rolling around and around. "That's good for your mental health."

"My mental health is fine, thank you. I'm the only normal one of the four of us."

"Which is, consequently, not good for your mental health."

"Did you just say 'consequently'?"

She tosses her hair over her shoulder. "I do know words, brother."

Upstairs, everything has gone very, very quiet. I hope they haven't killed Gideon. That would really put a damper on my birthday. I wonder if we'd name the new baby after him.

I say, "Listen, we're going to need to eat *something*. Let me warm up the turkey."

She crosses her arms. "Okay . . ."

"What?"

"You're being a fucking drama queen. Mom and Dad'll be down in a second, they'll apologize for yelling, and we'll all eat together. And don't you dare say *Not all of us because Noah isn't here waaaah*."

I tackle her and smother her under my arm. "We're playing house!" I tell her. "Feeding our children."

"Preggers, Deafy, and . . . what's Dad? Hopelessly Dreamy."

"I never should have let you name them."

"I think they're beautiful names."

"They're going to get beat up in kindergarten."

"Like they'll ever be mature enough for kindergarten."

I should make *something* to eat. "Hey, didn't we have another kid . . . ?"

"Oh, Moses? He ran away. Across the Red Sea."

I have my head in the refrigerator, looking for some kind of vegetable—our children might never pass preschool, but they'll be well-fed, goddamn it—when Claudia goes, "Uh, Chase?"

Gideon's running down the stairs, signing **Baby baby baby**.

"What?" I say, with my hands and with my voice all at the same time.

"Oh, my God," Claudia says.

My heart's in 3/4 time. "Wait, seriously?"

Claudia's way better at simultaneously signing and speaking. "Mom's having the baby?"

Gideon nods and flops down at the bottom of the stairs. **Baby hospital birthday!**

My boy is so smart sometimes.

We're still gaping like we didn't know Mom was pregnant when Mom and Dad come downstairs. Mom looks totally fine. I expected her to be dripping or something.

"I'm going to go ahead and bring her to the hospital," Dad says. "I'll be back soon, okay?" He kisses my cheek. "Fix them something to eat?"

"Okay. Okay." I can't quit smiling, and it's ridiculous. "Congratulations."

"Thank you, Chase." He swipes his finger over the bridge of my nose and looks at Mom as she kisses Gideon and Claude good-bye. "I'm just going to drop her off and get her comfortable and I'll be back, okay?"

"Wait, what?" I shake my head. "Stay with her."

"It's your birthday. We're not going to forget about you. Mom and I agreed this is best, okay?"

Mom kisses the top of my head. "Probably the last birthday you won't share with your sister, too."

I smile and choke out "Thank you." I have no idea what I'm thanking her for. I sign **Say bye** to Gideon.

Bye hospital bye baby.

Claudia rolls her eyes. "Boy doesn't even know what he's saying good-bye to." **Hello baby.**

"I'll take care of the kids," I say, pulling Claudia under my arm to shut her up. "Don't worry about their demon-asses." I smile. "And when you get back we'll cut the cake, Dad, okay?"

I put the turkey in the oven, put in a movie, and try to relax, but it's hard when my mind is a blur of Gideon's hands saying *baby*. When Newbaby is more than just a few stitches on the guitar strap Noah gave me.

And Noah. Is. Less.

Gideon found a squirt gun in the toy box and is now shooting air at me and Claudia.

"No Camus quote for the occasion, Chase?" Claudia asks.

I wrack. "Um . . . okay. *L'Etranger*."

"Hmm?"

"*What did other people's deaths or a mother's love matter to*

66

me; what did his God or the lives people choose or the fate they think they elect matter to me when we're all elected by the same fate, me and billions of privileged people like him who also called themselves my brothers? Couldn't he see, couldn't he see that? Everybody was privileged. There were only privileged people.'" I decide to end the quote there, swallowing the bit that says we are all condemned. Noah, I know, would never allow this false happy ending. But Noah isn't here.

Claudia's looking at me blankly. "What about people without beach houses?"

The turkey's twenty minutes burned before the fire alarm clues us in. "Shit!" I shout, wafting smoke out of the oven while Claudia stands on a chair and engages in combat with the alarm. "Christ, Claude, you're a girl! Aren't you supposed to have a gene for this?'

"Ask *Gideon*! He's the one with heightened senses!"

Leaning out the window and aiming his water gun at the constellations, oblivious to the noise, Gideon looks about as heightened as a headless chicken.

"Okay," Claudia says, covering one ear with her shoulder. "Um, we can just eat fruit for dinner?"

"Or cake," I say.

"Shitdamn!" Dad's voice goes. "What happened here?"

"Dad!" Claudia and I shout, and Claudia throws the lid

of the smoke detector's battery compartment toward Gid so he'll turn around.

Dad stumbles in from the landing, unnecessary jacket halfway off.

"Turns out none of us have the cooking gene," I say.

Dad stands beside me and peers into the oven. "Shit. Damn. Was there food in here, or did you start off baking soot?"

"Okay, I know, fail. I guess we could—"

"How's Mom?" Claudia says.

"Juuust fine." Dad wipes his hands on his jeans. "She's still got quite a while left. We should have time to do your birthday and still all get over there. And without making Gid bear the waiting room for too long."

"Any news from Noah?" I say.

"Not a word. That cell phone plan was just money down the drain, eh? Gideon!"

He's standing on a chair to reach the counter, eating frosting off my cake. I say, "Grab him, Claude!"

She scoops him up and smacks his back systematically until he cries.

"Can't you shut that off?" Dad asks, and I hope he means the smoke detector, not Gid, or he's going to have tons of fun having a new baby around. Thankfully, he breathes his sigh of relief when I find the right wire to pull, even though Gid's still hollering.

"Look," I say. "Let's just go to the hospital. There's a little cafeteria there, yeah? We can even find some cake or something there, I bet."

"You are *not* eating hospital food on your birthday." Dad pulls me under his arm. "Come on, kids. Let's get out of here before the fire department comes. Who wants pizza?"

I sign **Pizza**, one of the *best* signs, to Gideon, and he stops crying and squirms out of Claudia's arms so he can dance. Dad laughs. "Well, you've told Gid. It's set in stone now!"

In the car, I turn on the summeriest radio station I can find and let the wind blow my sweat off. None of us talks, but it's like we're buzzing; I can see *Newbaby Newbaby Newbaby* vibrating in all of our minds. Well, maybe not Gideon's, since he's staring out the window signing **pizza** to himself.

We pass by the first three pizza places without even slowing down, and I don't understand why until I look at the clock. Eleven fifteen. On a Tuesday, nothing's open.

"We can just go to the hospital," I mumble to him.

"It's your birthday, Chase. I'm not ruining it."

"It's Newbaby's birthday too."

Dad looks at me and wrinkles his nose. "What'd you call her?"

"It's Noah's name." I close my eyes. "Seriously. I don't want to do this. I want to be at the hospital."

"This selfless thing is not going to work on me, kid."

"You know I'm not selfless." I'm just like him, after all.

We park outside the greasiest pizza place, and Claudia and Gideon and I lean against the building while my father pulls on the door. "Come on," he growls to the lock. "Come *on*."

"It's closed." I say.

"We need pizza." He keeps tugging. "It's your *birthday*." The streetlights shine on his cheeks, highlighting his laugh lines.

"It's *closed*!" I step into the dark, away from the restaurant. "It already . . ." *Noah's gone.* "It's already been ruined, Dad. It's *over*."

Claudia picks up Gideon like she's preparing to run with him.

Dad drops his hands to his sides. "Chase . . ." he starts, quietly, then raises his arms and drops them again. "Chase."

I wipe my nose. "Your cell phone's ringing."

He digs his phone out of his pocket, and we all watch his face melt into the—"Darling, I'm so sorry, I so meant to be there"—and then relax and smile as he goes, "Okay. Okay. We're coming."

He slaps the phone shut and cuddles us up. "She's here, kids! She's here!"

Claudia translates for Gideon as fast as she can. Gideon jumps up and down and signs **Bye hospital more baby here!**

"Don't be upset, Chase," Dad whispers to me.

I'm smiling and crying all at once, and it's so hot, but the wind's taking tears away like they're sweat.

"She's healthy?" I say.

"She's perfect."

Gideon's dancing, and Claudia's dancing too, which is nice, even though hers is weird and sexualized. They sparkle in the lights of the no-pizza place, and my father is holding my arms, waiting for me to dance too, waiting for me to dance so he can.

And because no one else is willing to play Noah, I drop my voice and I say it, I ask, "Can she hear?"

16TH SUMMER

SEVEN

I can't believe it's been a year since we've been to the beach. We really need to start doing trips during the off-season, but I didn't even think to suggest it this year. It would have been too much trouble to travel with the baby. This road trip down to the beach is Lucy's first long car ride, and it's brutal for all of us, even though she's almost a year old and should be past her bitchiest phase. I'm glad we didn't try it when she was still colicky.

Because she screams. The entire time. At one point, Claudia says that if she does not get out of this car, she is going to explode all over us, and we will drown in her insides. We'll die choking on bits of her large intestines. She doesn't say this bit, but I can picture it.

Noah leans back and gives me a look. *"There is no fate that cannot be surmounted by scorn."*

"Do you boys have Camus's entire body of work memorized?" quips my father.

"Just me and Noah," I say. "Not Gideon."

Gideon is the only one who isn't totally fed up with the baby. He's fascinated by everything about her—her little feet, her smile, her curls. The one thing he doesn't notice is the thing that never fails to make us smile—the way she looks over when we call her name. We've basically been shouting "Lucy" at her for a year now. She hears! She turns her head! Magic baby.

Claudia leans her head against my shoulder. "Wake me up when we get there."

Lucy shrieks again, and I close my eyes. "I don't know if we're going to live that long."

"Okay. Wake me up when I'm dead."

"Just open yourself to the gentle indifference of the world," Noah advises.

Dad says, "Christ."

"Now, now." Mom rubs her childless stomach.

Hungry, Gideon says.

I say, "Mom, Gid's hungry."

She cranes her neck back and tries to sign to Gideon, but he's all the way in the back with Lucy, and she can't catch his eye. "Claudia, tell him I'll make spaghetti when we get to the house."

"Spaghetti at the beach?" Noah raises an eyebrow.

Claudia says, "He doesn't know the signs, Mom." Around February, Claudia officially refused to stop translating for Gideon—about two months after Gideon officially refused to learn any new signs.

"I sign better than he does," Claudia had said. "This is ridiculous."

I turn around and tap his knee. **Food soon.**

Food me food Lucy food food food Gideon signs, and he shakes Lucy's rattle in her face.

Claudia's watching him with a frown. When I catch her, she looks away and presses her cheek against the window. "He baby-signs," she says. "He's *seven.*"

"I know," Noah says.

"It's not cute anymore."

"I know," Mom says.

"We just need to support him," Dad says. "His tutor thinks he's making good progress, he just needs full support."

"He needs a Deaf school," Mom says.

Dad clears his throat. "And we need to be able to afford Noah's tuition without paying twice as much for elementary school."

"Stop it," Claudia and I say together.

Noah angsts up and plays with his fingernails, the same way he does when anyone talks about college. Even though he liked his freshman year okay, since we heard Melinda dropped out, college is this weird competition. Not only does Noah have to stay past the middle of his sophomore year to beat her, but he also has to be happy. "Unfortunately," Noah told me once while he was poring over textbooks, "these things might not coexist."

"Camus?" I asked.

"McGill. I think I'm learning to be articulate or something."

Mom thinks Noah doesn't like college because he's living at home, so he agreed he'd try living on campus next year. I'm really, really not happy about this. Last summer, I took it for granted that Noah was leaving. When he decided last-minute to keep living at home, I felt a kind of relief that I'm not willing to give up now.

Mom and Dad are still arguing about Deaf school and college and Noah and everything when we get to the house and start unpacking, but it's hard to care when the day's this hot. It's hard to care about much of anything besides when I'm getting in the ocean. I'm clearly not the only one who feels this way, because when I'm hoisting Lucy's car seat up the steps, I realize Gid's totally gone.

"Gideon!"

There he is, sprinting toward the waterline. "Someone grab him!" Dad shouts.

"He's *seven*," Noah says under his breath, but takes off after him before we can all scream about how he'll get dizzy.

Lugging this car seat is more trouble than it's worth, so I say, "All right, Luce," and free her from all the buckles and chains and shackles. She smiles at me. "Yeah, I bet you're happy." I kiss her forehead and scoop her back up. Lucy basically has a master's degree in being carried. She holds on like nothing I've ever seen. Love it.

I unlock the front door with my free side while Lucy clings to the other. "Welcome home, Lucy," I whisper to her.

"Forget something?"

I turn around in the doorway, and there's the college dropout herself, holding Lucy's car seat, that smile on those perfectly glossed lips.

I sort of expected her to be depressed, mumbling

incoherently. I guess this is the way you picture someone when you hear they had some horrific experience and then a nervous breakdown, but you don't hear any specifics.

"Hey, Melinda."

She leans forward and kisses Lucy's chubby and cracker-crumbed cheek. "She got *huge*!"

"Nah, she's a peanut. She has a lot of hair, though." Right now it's pulled into curly pigtails. Brown hair. Claudia and Dad and I are now officially the blond minority.

Melinda follows me inside, car seat dangling from her hand. The house looks slightly different. The renters moved the furniture.

"How long have you been here?" I ask, while my parents come in and hug her and tell her how glad they are she's feeling better. I think maybe what happened was she got sick or something during the year, but no one's really explained it to me. A few times, I'm sure I've walked in on Noah discussing it with our parents, but they always shut up too quickly for me to follow what's going on. Maybe it's drugs.

"Came in two nights ago," she says. That's so weird. We're supposed to get in the same day as the Hathaways, kind of magically. We always have before.

"Where's—"

"Shannon's having lunch." She jerks her thumb back

80

toward her house and points, strangely, with her tongue. "He'll be over here soon." She looks at me. "Bella's at ballet camp."

"She's not coming at all?" Claudia says, also looking at me.

"Not this summer."

I want to feel sad about this, and I do, in a way, but a bigger part of me than I'd like to admit is relieved. I don't regret kissing Bella, but it does feel like something I did when I was a lot younger. It feels like a conversation we never finished, and I think it's been too long to pick it back up. It's not the greatest situation, but it's not as if Bella is my girlfriend, so maybe it's better for both of us to just let it go. We're not fourteen anymore.

Noah comes in, dragging sandy Gideon. "Child needs food," he says. "He's some sort of hungry Gideon-monster." He kisses Melinda's cheek, so quickly I almost miss it, on the way to the refrigerator to unpack the sodas from the cooler.

My parents have already claimed beers and are outside on the balcony, talking to each other with their bodies fully facing the sea. I wonder which one of them would jump first.

"We've got to baby-proof this place," I say, when Lucy tries to pull up on the table and cries when she can't.

"Baby-proofing's so she doesn't get hurt," Noah says. "It's not for her bruised ego."

Claudia covers her ears and leans over the counter. "I cannot take any more of this screaming," she says. She kicks off Gideon, who's tugging at her jeans to see if she's okay because the ear-covering concept completely confuses him, I guess. I make a funny face at him, and he laughs and makes one back.

"Let's get out." Noah shuts the refrigerator. "Downtown. We'll sunscreen the kids, put them on the beach, tell Mom and Dad they have no choice but to watch them. It'll be cake. Claudia, tell Gideon to go put his bathing suit on."

Claudia says, "I am not translating for Gideon until he *learns how to say 'bathing suit.'*"

Gideon. I grab his shoulder. **Swim beach yes?**

Yes he says, and runs to his room where I've hauled his little suitcase. I shrug at Claudia. "It's not that difficult. . . ."

"It's not about difficult."

Melinda snaps open a soda, and the hiss reminds us that, if Claudia and I are going to play house, we should do better than Mom and Dad and not argue in front of people who don't want to hear it.

"Baby sunscreen's in the red bag," I say.

Noah gets Lucy in her new bathing suit, and she shrieks while we put sunscreen on her. Claudia looks like her head's about to explode, so I say, "Claude, go get Shannon, okay?"

She comes back with him, and I can tell she's way more

impressed than I am that he grew about six inches over the year and got some sort of beard-in-training. But he gives me that big smile and says, "How's it going, soldier?" so I'll forgive the drippy way he and my sister are eyeing each other when they think I'm not looking. It seems so weird that they're still doing their imitation of dating even though Bella and I have finished.

Once the kids are ready, Noah brings them to Mom and Dad on the balcony and says, "Can you watch these two? We're going out."

"Oh." Mom turns around, doing that plastic smile. "Oh, wait! We need a family photo first!"

I raise an eyebrow at Dad while Mom rushes through the bags, looking for the camera. *"What?"* I say.

Dad drains the rest of his beer. "I don't know. Let's just do it."

I say, "But—"

"I guess she thinks this is important or something. I don't know, Chase. It's easier just to do it than ask questions."

Melinda offers to take the picture, so the eight of us traipse out to the sand outside the beach house. To be out here in my real clothes always feels a bit like sacrilege—like I'm not showing the beach the respect it deserves.

"All riiiight," Melinda says. "Mr. and Mrs. McGill, sit in the back, okay?"

When my parents have to sit in the sand without a towel, they always look like they think they're going to get a disease. Mom, of course, has the worried face, while my father looks like a disease might be a nice change of pace.

"Then Noah right in front, Claudia and Chase on either side of them, then Gideon and Lucy—Chase, grab Gideon, he's running off."

I snatch Gideon up and set him on my lap.

"And Claudia, you hold Lucy—"

"I don't want to hold Lucy."

"Claudia," Dad says. "Hold your sister."

Noah shakes his head and takes the baby.

"And here we go." Melinda says. "One, two, three—" She lowers the camera and fake-applauds. "Very nice. Gorgeous family."

Claudia stretches over Noah and Lucy and kisses my cheek. I watch Melinda, who's studying the picture on the camera's screen with that look of longing that makes me wish we'd given up and argued in front of her.

Don't look at us like we're a picture.

We're really not.

By the time we finally escape downtown, Claudia's leapfrogging empty benches and full benches and dancing in the gutters, she's so happy to be free. I'm trying to catch Shannon up on my life, and realizing, like always, that there's not much to say. Nothing's happened to me that can't be attributed to these summers.

Shannon, on the other hand, has been actually living. He has a girlfriend, much to Claudia's dismay, and a first-choice college and a job at an art supply store back at home. He has all these things I figured were for people who didn't have the McGills and the Hathaways and the beach house.

"You should get a job," Shannon says. "Seriously, it's awesome."

"What do I need a job for?"

"Money, soldier." Shannon rubs his fingers together. "Chicks."

I don't know what that gesture has to do with girls, but okay.

I say, "What's Bella doing at camp?"

"Preparing for some recital or something." Shannon chews on a fingernail. "She's hoping to get a scholarship somewhere, so she has to start working toward it now."

"Jesus."

"She's a good dancer, you know that."

I say, "Yeah."

"She told me to tell you hi."

"Cool." I shrug and stuff my hands in my pockets. "So, yeah. It's not going to happen. The career thing."

"A summer job is not exactly a commitment," Shannon says.

"I don't want to work all summer. That's so . . . grown-up."

Melinda laughs and slips her arm around Noah's waist. "Chase Everboy McGill."

I say, "I still don't get what that means."

She grins. "Forever young, forever nervous, forever sixteen."

"*Evening's slight anxiety in a sixteen-year-old heart,*" Noah mumbles to her.

Melinda turns to him in mock horror. "*Consuming one by one over a period of months the victims stretched out in the form of crosses on the beach at the deathlike hour of noon!*"

I say, "Oh, shut up, I'm not even sixteen yet."

"You only have to be fifteen to work down here," Shannon says, completely misunderstanding what we're talking about; he never got into Camus. He says, "How can I make this more kid-friendly for you?" He points. "Look, Candy Kitchen's hiring. Fill out an app, okay? Gideon will love the free candy, and we'll waste every cent you earn at the arcade, I promise. Zero accountability required."

I look at Noah and Melinda and Claudia. "What do you guys think?"

"Do it," Noah says, kissing Melinda's cheek. "It'll keep you out of our hair for a little while."

"Mmm-hmm." Claudia's distracted, but I can't figure out what she's looking at. I guess a job is better than trying to keep track of her all summer, trailing behind like I'm the younger sibling, or watching Noah and Melinda get too handsy whenever they think I'm not looking. And it doesn't seem like I'm ever going to get to see Shannon unless I'm punching the clock alongside him. Damn it. Whatever happened to building sand castles? Maybe coming downtown today was a mistake.

It takes forever to get an application and get it filled out; I have to call Mom and Dad to get my social security number, then explain to them why I'm applying for a job, which requires Shannon to explain to me, again, why I'm applying for a job. By the time Shannon and I get out of there, Melinda, Noah, and Claude are nowhere to be seen, and we're frickin' starving.

It's four slices of pizza later when my cell phone rings. It's Noah's number, and I barely recognize it. I don't have his number saved because he hates his cell phone and *never* uses it.

"Hello?"

"Uh, Chase? Can you get down to the boardwalk? We . . . have a situation."

Usually "we have a situation" means *the baby will not stop crying* or *Gideon threw up on the floor* or *Claudia's in trouble with the police.*

Shit. "What'd she do?"

"Umm . . ."

I hang up. "Shannon, man, we got to get to the boardwalk."

He tosses his cup into the trash can. "Whatever you say, kid."

We sprint across the street to the boardwalk and follow it until we see Claudia getting blasted by some rent-a-cop. Noah and Melinda are standing by—her face is buried in his shirt, and I think she's crying before I hear her giggling.

Then I see two wet circles on the front of Claudia's T-shirt.

Rent-a-Cop says, "It's just a point of public decency, young lady. You gotta understand that this is a family beach, that there are *families* that can see you."

Melinda snorts into Noah's shirt.

I say, "Christ, Claude, what did you do?"

Rent-a-Cop turns to me. "It's a matter of public decency, kid—"

"I just went swimming." Claudia points down the beach. "There were these girls and they asked me to swim with them, so I just took off my shirt and went swimming with them."

"Claudia!"

She looks at me with her arms raised. "Chase, come on, it was perfectly okay! I kept my shorts on! I had a bra."

"A *white* bra," Rent-a-Cop specifies.

Noah totally loses it at this point and has to let go of Melinda, he's laughing so hard. Shannon has this look on his face like he doesn't know us and doesn't know this is the kind of situation we get in. That sort of pisses me off. Half the time, he's in trouble with us, after all. I'm not saying this is ideal, but shouldn't he be used to it by now?

This seagull totally starts yelling at us.

"Look," I say. "She's twelve years old, she wasn't naked, and she . . . has no other public exposure citations." *Please don't check that.* "She gets off with a warning, yeah?"

Rent-a-Cop puffs up. "I'd really like to speak with your parents."

I pull Claudia toward me. "They're at home with the new baby and our deaf brother. Honestly, please don't bother them with this. Please." I grip Claudia hard enough to bruise her shoulder. "We'll punish her sufficiently. Promise."

We start hitting her the second we're free. "What were you thinking?" Shannon says. "Taking off your clothes with random girls?"

Melinda snorts. "Yeah, you should talk."

89

Claudia says, "They were cute! They wanted to swim! I wanted to have fun!"

I shove Noah. "Why weren't you watching her?"

Noah looks at Melinda. "Uhh . . ."

"Noah!"

"She's twelve, Chase. The reason we left the kids at home was so we wouldn't have to do any babysitting. So we could just, like, be."

So Noah wouldn't have to run away.

Claudia says, "I was *fine*. I don't need someone to watch me. It was just stupid bad luck with a stupid fucking cop."

I lean on Shannon's shoulder. "This is just like last year. Except escalated. Next year we'll be pulling Claudia out of a swampy bog or something. A swampy bog full of sex."

Noah rolls his eyes. "And the year before, and the year before, and the year before, and the year after and after . . ."

"*'And ever the same sky through the years,'*" Melinda and I say, together.

"You guys are spooky," Shannon says.

Claudia climbs onto my back, and her stupid wet twelve-year-old boobs press into my shirt. Noah rolls his eyes and holds Melinda close, but she's looking at me, so I look at the sky.

EIGHT

*A*re they making you nervous?" my father asks. He stands next to me at the railing on the balcony where we watch everyone rushing around on the beach like lightning bugs.

"They *always* make me nervous."

He smiles. "Me too."

Down on the sand, Noah's flashlight hits Gideon. "I found you!" he shouts. He turns the flashlight on himself so Gideon can see him sign **find find find.**

"Next year Lucy'll be running around with them," I say. "Just one more to watch."

Lucy's currently showing off how well she can stand, clinging on to the bars on my other side. I swing my guitar back around to my chest and strum for a little while, making up chord progressions as I go along.

Dad says, "Stuff might be different next year, Chase."

I laugh. "Stuff is never different. Where's Mom?"

"Buying more ice-cream sandwiches. Shannon ate them all."

"Yeah, Shannon would."

He tucks me under his arm. "You okay? You seem quiet."

I concentrate on my fingers. "Yeah, traveling just tires me out." I shrug. "I'm fine."

"Glad to hear it."

"Ahhh," Lucy says, and I pick her up so she can see over the railing. For a second, the three of us just stand there, listening to all of them scream—Claudia and Gideon most of all, with a scattered giggle from Melinda.

"God, Gideon's voice," Dad says.

I laugh. "I know."

"It just . . . makes you completely aware of how self-conscious the rest of us sound, doesn't it?"

"Ha, yeah."

"We've got to do something about his signing, though." Dad shakes his head. "Or there's going to be no way to talk your mom out of a Deaf school for him."

"House would be damn still with both him and Noah living at school."

"You'd have to play us more songs."

I say, "I know."

The flashlight beams crisscross and one finally hits Claudia. "Got you!" Shannon screams.

"Aw, goddamn it."

I sling my guitar over my shoulder—it's still on the strap Noah gave me—and hitch Lucy up my hip and squeeze her tight. "I'm going to take her down to the beach," I say. Lucy, so far, hasn't liked the sand much, and this is a problem. A problem only constant exposure is going to fix. She's a McGill. She'll like the sand.

"Keep an eye on her," Dad says.

I turn and look at him. "Of course."

He smiles a little. "Of course."

I take Lucy down the stairs and into the sand. I figure I'll set up camp under the house—that way she won't mess up the game, and I can see her well enough in the beams from their flashlights—and I run right into Melinda.

I stutter, "Oh, hey."

I can just barely see her smile. "Oh, hey, Chase."

She sits down in the sand next to me and we watch Lucy crawl. "Does she walk yet?" Melinda asks.

I play a few notes. "Not really. She can stand and pull up and everything, but she's not really walking. Unless we hold her hands."

"Does she talk?"

I say, "Luce, what's my name?"

"Aaaaase."

I smile. "That's about it."

"It's nice she can hear."

"Really no reason, logically, that she shouldn't be able to hear. Gid was kind of, just . . . a random fluke."

"Probably something got messed up when he was embryonic. Your mom drank, right?"

I look at her, not that it makes any difference. We're just silhouettes. Lucy's patting noises in the sand are the only way I know she hasn't disappeared. The boys and Claudia keep swinging beams like searchlights over the beach.

I say, "How can you ask me that?"

"Well, it helped that it was a rhetorical question."

I reach out and grab Lucy's ankle, and she shrieks. I smile and let her go, play a few bars of a folk song.

She says, "I was studying child development. You know. Before I left school."

"Why'd you leave?"

She pulls her knees up, and I see deeper shadows in the

shallow sand where her legs used to be. "Stuff happened. Stuff that made me not feel like staying."

I feel like covering Lucy's ears. Or playing so loud she can't hear. "Oh."

We're quiet, lying in the sand, watching the stars, while Lucy crawls slow circles around us. I drop a few more notes.

I say, "Can I ask you something?"

She exhales. "Of course, Chase."

"What's the deal with you and Noah?"

She laughs. "What's the deal with *you* and Noah?"

"Uh, he's my brother. He runs, I watch."

"Same here. Except for the brother bit. What about you and Bella?"

I exhale. It feels like I haven't seen Bella in years. I can't even begin to remember what she tastes like. I've kissed girls at home since I've kissed her. Bella was a lifetime ago, but I don't want to feel that way. It was one year. I shouldn't feel so goddamn disconnected.

I just say, "Um, there's nothing going on with me and Bella."

"Not when she's not here, right?"

I hear Melinda move, but it takes me a second to realize she's now on her side, facing me. Her mouth is two inches away from my mouth. Her body's pressed against my guitar.

Her fingers are touching someone's embroidered name, but I can't see well enough to tell whose.

I choke out, "Lucy, are you close?"

"Co," she says.

Close.

I whisper, "I should check on Gideon."

"Gideon's fine," she says.

We're both inching toward each other, millimeter by millimeter, both too afraid I'll run away if we try for something more final, more dramatic. I want to say out loud that I'm Chase, and I don't run away, even when I should, but then her mouth is on mine and I can't talk.

This isn't like any kiss I've ever had. I feel like she's trying to breathe the air out of my lungs. I'm pushing my hands into her body without meaning to, and I feel like I could fall all the way through her. I'm Alice in Wonderland, and that's maybe the stupidest thing I've ever thought.

She's still kissing me. No, it's too big, too dramatic, Noah could see, Noah could be upset—I pull away.

"What's wrong?" she says.

My first thought is *You're old*.

I say, "You're doing something with Noah. I can't . . . and I have some weird innocent not-thing going on with Bella—"

"Bella's not here."

"She still exists."

"So you're going to wait your whole life for her?"

I'm going to wait my whole summers for her. I say, "I can't be sitting here, kissing you, and my baby sister's right here, and . . ."

She's still so close to me. How is she so close to me?

She says, *"Nothing is true that forces one to exclude."*

I can't breathe too well.

"So don't exclude yourself, Chase." She lays her head on my shoulder. "God, I just want something—anything—that's real."

From that point on, all I can think about is *kissing*. And it's like it's *everywhere*. Noah and Melinda in the rain. Mom and Dad after they fight. Even in Gideon and Lucy's stupid cartoons, kissing! The only person who isn't kissing is Claudia; I would have expected she'd be on Shannon by now, but he's apparently devoted to his girlfriend back home, and Claude's making this big deal out of being heartbroken.

Bella never made me feel this way. Bella was just lips. We're talking about whole bodies, now. We're talking about lungs.

I'm just confused. Suddenly everything has this *subtext*. I'm beginning to understand what Noah meant about foreplay. I think my whole life is foreplay. The girls lying on their stomachs on the beach every day? It doesn't matter if they're six or sixteen or sixty. It's sex. Girls are sex! I feel like I've opened up a Pandora's box of adolescence full of sunlight and lip gloss and Camus.

Noah says, "Seriously, Chase, what's gotten into you?"

"The idea that the female race extends beyond Bella and my sisters."

Noah laughs. "The things you discover when you live your life on beaches."

I know I'm only fifteen, but I'm going to bed every night terrified that I'm going to die a virgin if I don't have sex *right now*. I don't think I've ever needed anything this badly. It's almost terrifying. I'm addicted to something I've never tried.

"Do you want to borrow a magazine?" Noah asks. "Or, like, an internet connection?"

But seriously, I'm afraid there's something wrong with me. There's this girl I work with, and before I would have thought she was cute and that would have been okay—but now? I feel like doing things with her. *To* her!

Her name is Joanna, and she always wears pink shirts underneath her white apron. She must have at least twenty pink shirts, I swear. She piles all her hair on top of her head, like every girl in the world, but it looks better on her. She doesn't wear makeup.

Once, when she was reaching for the gummi worms, and I was going for the wax bottles, the inside of her wrist touched the top of my hand. I got an erection immediately. It was horrible. I had to serve the next set of customers with my crotch pressed against the cash register.

And that's just one of the things that's hard about working.

Because my lack of sex isn't even my only problem. I wish. What's worse, honestly, is just the fact that I'm working when every instinct in me tells me I'm supposed to be out on the beach. All the people come in midday, sandy and sunburned, and I just want to say, *Why are you here? Why are you downtown when you should be on the ocean?* but my boss says all I'm allowed to say is, "Hi, can I help you?"

Claudia starts calling me *Chase face*, which I think has something to do with me not smiling as much as I usually do. Mom keeps wanting to *talk*, but whenever I take her up on it, all she does is act bored and tell me how wrong I am, which Dad says is a defense mechanism, but really, it's just very irritating.

"I feel like I'm throwing the summer away," I tell her.

She's painting her nails with exaggerated precision. "No one made you get a job, Chase."

"I hate being grown-up," I say, trying not to picture Melinda's mouth around *Chase Everboy McGill*.

Actually, I spend a lot of time trying not to picture Melinda's mouth. Why is it so different from everybody else's mouth? How does she get the left side higher than the right side when she smiles? One time, I actually catch myself trying to imitate it in the mirror. And getting turned on by it. Seriously, something is very wrong with me.

"Oh, hey, I got an e-mail from Bella," Shannon tells me at work one day. We're on break, and Melinda stopped by to sample all the fudge with us. Except they're doing most of the sampling, and I'm organizing the stuffed animals, again, so I don't have to watch Melinda lick her fingers.

"Just thought you'd be interested," he says.

"Oh. Cool."

"She got the lead in some performance they're doing. She gets to be in pointe shoes, I guess, so she's excited."

I should be picturing Bella's feet in pointe shoes, long and lean and perfect.

"Isn't that lovely, Chase?" Melinda says, her voice slow and syrupy. I will not look at her. I will not check if her mouth is full.

"Yeah," I croak out. "Awesome."

I'm hanging up my apron after work that day, still struggling to get that goddamn voice to stop playing in my ears, when

Mom calls my cell phone. She says, "Could you find your brother, please?"

"Uh, which one?"

"*Both* of them. I made an appointment with a speech therapist here she's supposed to be fantastic—and Noah was supposed to have Gideon there an hour ago. And she just called and says she's waiting around in her office with no sign of them."

"How do you expect me to find him?"

"Can you please be Can-Do Chase and not Sullen Chase?"

Oh, all right.

Tracking down Noah is, honestly, not that hard. Most of the time when he runs away now, he's with Melinda. So I call Shannon.

"I know he thinks the speech-therapy thing is stupid." Shannon's on the beach—I can hear the waves. I want to tell him bringing a cell phone out to the beach with you is so not okay, but I'm afraid he'll hang up. Or leave the beach.

"Yeah, he would. When'd you see him last?"

"He and Melinda had lunch together like an hour ago. Uh, Melinda?"

I listen to him talk to her for a minute, try not to strain to hear her voice, try to cover my ears, try to *not picture her mouth.*

"He told Melinda he's taking Gideon to the swings?"

"Thanks, Shannon."

The park's right downtown, just down the parking lot and across the street from where I work. As soon as I get to the end of the lot, I see Noah pushing Gideon in his favorite swing.

Problem is, Noah sees me, too. By the time I've climbed over the gate into the playground, Noah's found a largish stick among the gravel and is brandishing it in my direction. "Help, help!" he calls when I keep coming toward him. "Candy Kitchen boy's trying to steal my baby!"

It's then that I realize I'm still wearing my white linen hat.

"Shitdamn." I take it off and crumple it in my hand. "Noah, come on. I'm sure Mom's paying, like, billions of dollars for this speech therapist."

"He doesn't *speak*. What does he need a fucking therapist for?"

"I'm sure she knows sign language. She can teach him new signs. Come on, man."

"He doesn't need new signs. This talking thing is bullshit, Chase. It's *bullshit*."

Shit. Noah's actually upset.

"Look." He returns to the swing, where Gideon's dragging his feet in the gravel. "*This* is communication," he says, wrapping his arms around Gideon's little body. "Learning more hand gestures to yell at him so he'll do what Dad or whatever wants him to do? *Not* communication."

"Yeah, and the speech therapist is going to take away your ability to hug Gideon. You've figured it all out."

Noah stuffs his hands in his pockets.

"Look," I say. "Stop pouting. Give me the directions and I'll take him, whatever, and you can run away and be happy. Okay? But don't teach him this split-when-it-gets-rough-or-doesn't-get-rough thing. Jesus, he's already too much like you."

"Ooh, inspirational speech much, *Dad*? You're reaaaally qualified to bitch about us turning into each other. *Shitdamn*."

I sigh.

"You don't have your license," he says.

"I can drive. Give me the fucking directions."

Noah picks Gideon up like he's Lucy's age. "You're not driving him without a license."

"Then come on."

He looks at Gideon.

"Noah, I'm not leaving. What are you going to do, run? I'm faster than you. Especially when I'm not weighed down by a seven-year-old."

"Fuck you, Chase."

"Come on."

I don't know how, in this, I convinced Noah, but in a second he's driving Gideon and me to the speech therapist. As if his only job is to prove everyone wrong, Gideon's babbling to himself in the backseat.

"He's happy," Noah says. "Happy to not make sense. And unlike everyone else, he knows he's not making sense."

I say, "Don't you think he'd be better off if he could talk more?"

"What does he need to say that he can't mime out for us?"

"Nothing now, Noah, he's seven goddamn years old. Christ. But . . . but what about when he's older? Trying to talk to a girl?"

"A deaf girl?"

"Either one." Though I can't picture Gideon with a hearing girl. "Sign or English, he's . . . not proficient."

"He has that *smile*. People just want to touch him. No words can compete with being the guy people just want to touch." Noah shakes his head. "You can live a nice life that way."

"Personal experience, much?"

"Personal experience this, Chase. He's my little brother and I want him to be happy, and I'm always happiest when people don't make me talk."

"What about when I make you talk?"

He's quiet for a minute. "Well, it's different with you."

"Why's that?"

"Because I love you, asshole."

I smile. "Ever consider that Gideon might love me too?"

"I guess it's a possibility. I actually never thought about . . . I mean, let's be honest, you're pretty unlovable. . . ."

"Uh-huh."

We park and unpack Gideon—he's still babbly. The speech therapist's office is identical to the rest of the buildings here—they all look old, but like they could be swept away at any minute by a stray wave. When we sit in the waiting room, Gideon between us, I flash back, weirdly, to taking my learner's permit test. I sat on that stupid bench for hours, watching the ads on the wall and wondering when the hell they were going to flash my number.

I'm even more nervous now. The longer we wait—ten minutes, then fifteen, then twenty—the more I feel myself growing a scowl to match Noah's.

The therapist's name is Miss Lyn or some shit like that, and she crouches down when she talks to us, like Noah wouldn't be a full foot taller than her if he stood up. "I'm just going to take Gideon back with me for a little while and see how he communicates," she says. "Why don't you boys stay here and fill out some forms, okay? And when Gideon and I are done, we'll all go over them together."

"He's totally deaf," Noah tells her. "Wouldn't hear if you shot a gun next to him."

Miss Lyn smiles. "Well. We'll take very good care of him, then."

"Born deaf," Noah says. "Can't lip-read at all."

"Lip-reading's a tough skill."

"His signing *sucks*, too."

"Well, maybe we can help with that."

This is so not the answer Noah's looking for, though God knows if there's anything that could make him happy at this point. He frowns hard at Miss Lyn as she takes Gideon's hand and brings him to a back room.

Soon we're both frowning hard at the paperwork. "Middle name?" Noah says. "Does Gideon even *have* a middle name?"

"I don't know."

Noah turns to me and says, "Do *you* have a middle name?" his glare implying that, if I do, this whole thing is somehow my fault.

"I . . . have no idea."

"Primary language spoken at home." Noah makes a face. "What does this mean? Our primary language? Gideon's? That's sort of why we're here. . . ."

"Um, it's under *family*, so I'm guessing ours?"

"Well . . ." Noah lowers his pen. The paperwork has defeated him. "What's our primary language?"

"English? ASL? Physical affection?"

"Food?" Noah says.

"Food's a good guess."

He picks up the pen. "I'm writing *food*, comma *passive aggressive*."

"Good call."

We've barely finished filling out the damn forms when Miss Lyn comes back with Gideon. Noah and I are instantly examining him, looking for tear marks or hand-shaped bruises, but he looks like our same stupid Gid.

Then she's talking to us.

"What we'd really like to do," she says, "is bring him up to a functional for-age ASL level. You expressed interest in keeping him in mainstream school?"

We nod.

"Then you might want to consider a cochlear implant, since his base hearing is near nonexistent. This obviously isn't for everyone, and it's quite expensive, even with insurance. But if you want him to have the closest to the stereotypically normal life, that's going to be your best option, though his hearing will probably never be equal to that of a person born hearing."

She puts her hand on his head. "Now, Gideon's obviously a very bright boy—"

She loses us here.

"—and we really just want to bring his language skills up to that level of intelligence."

"He doesn't have to act like a hearing boy," I say. "We like him how he is."

"A normal, hearing lifestyle doesn't have to be your goal," she tells us. "In fact, I'm relieved if it isn't. A normal, comfortable lifestyle for a Deaf boy could be a fantastic thing for him. What you need to do—"

Then she starts giving us names. ASL tutors who can help him. Videos that will improve his sign language. Ways to get him involved in the community. Methods that have proven helpful in cases like Gideon. Counselors for families with deaf kids.

It really doesn't seem fair to me. I think if a kid is born deaf, he should be born to learn sign language. It's the only way that makes sense. And I don't know what Noah's thinking, but I'm pretty sure he also thinks this isn't okay.

I wanted a solution. I wanted someone to flick a switch in Gideon's brain that would make him want to talk to us, make him cut off his ears and throw them at us if it would make us listen to him. I wanted proof that Gideon gives a shit, or that he should give a shit, and I'm leaving with a list of tutors.

A list of more people who will tell me how much work my brother needs.

Noah's upset again. I notice it more quickly this time, while he's buckling Gideon into the car.

"Gid's going to be fine," I tell him. "We'll make sure."

Noah climbs into the driver's seat and buckles his seat belt. *"Nobody realizes that some people expend tremendous energy merely to be normal,"* he says, his voice really tired, like he's been running a million miles.

He gets like this more often now, ever since he started college. He said living at home was to save money, but the choice not to move out was so insanely out of character for him that I have to think that there was some bigger reason. And I think it's this—part of Noah recognized that leaving all of us, really, finally, permissibly, would be the complete and total end of him. Hell, spending every day an hour away on campus drained some of the life out of him. Maybe Noah doesn't cling because he loves us or run away because he doesn't. Maybe he clings because we're the only part of him that feels anything, and he runs because that anything is too much to stand.

I wonder if Melinda ever makes him cry.

"Do you want to stop for ice cream or something?" I ask, because that's what Dad always suggests when I'm upset.

"I'm tired, Chase," he says. "Let's just go home?"

I say okay, even though I know that as soon as we get there, he's going to go out for some run and not come back for a few hours or a few days. Because he hates us, and he hates us because he hates loving us. And maybe I'm deluding myself by thinking that Noah loves me the most—it's probably Gideon, who Noah would talk for in a heartbeat, if he asked, or it might even be Mom—but I don't think it's a stretch to say he hates me the most with that part of him that doesn't know how to need anyone.

Because I'm the one who should have been named Stay, and he's the one who should have been named Chase. And I came along and stole everything from him. I was the first one to make Noah McGill give a shit. And I pay for that every day, when I miss him.

"It's going to be okay," I say. "I promise."

In the backseat, Gideon signs **home Claudia Mom Dad beach cake**.

NINE

At least once, every time we're down here, we try to get everyone dressed up and go have a nice dinner somewhere off the boardwalk. This was hard enough before Newbaby, by virtue of Noah and Gid. Claudia and I love dressing up—it's one of the few things we have in common with Mom—but the boys are always such a hassle. As soon as we have them both dressed, one of them will slip off and return a second later in sandy shorts and flip-flops. Dad hates it too, but I think Mom whips him into submission somehow. His bow tie is his dog collar.

Tonight, Mom's too busy dressing Lucy to chase Gideon

and Noah into dress shirts and khakis, so I'm assigned to the big kid and Claudia's assigned to the little one.

"Yeah, because this really needs to be our priority." Noah wrestles with his tie like it's alive. "Dressing up and forking over two hundred dollars so Gideon can pick at his chicken nuggets and Claudia can order something she can't pronounce. Yeah, this is really at the top of our Need to Do list."

I think Noah sees some crisis I'm not aware of, like we're all supposed to be out saving the world right now instead of eating dinner.

I shut Camus and lay the book on the bed. "All right, bitch. Come here."

He stands in front of me, messing with his cuffs. "We're falling apart. Maybe Mom and Dad could, I don't know, talk to us?"

"I thought talking was uuuuuuuseless."

"Yeah, it's useless with *us* because we don't *say* anything."

"God, stop being Melinda." I tug Noah down to my level so I can do up his tie.

"Without Melinda, you'd have no Camus."

I exhale. "I know." I know it to my fucking bones.

He tugs the tie underneath his collar. "Look. We should just tell Mom and Dad that we want to actually discuss this, right?"

"Discuss what, exactly?"

"You know . . ."

The problem is that I do know, even if I don't think the growing tension between our parents is quite the tragedy Noah's making it out to be. "That's what we should do?" he says.

"Probably."

"Then how come we're not going to do it?"

There are a lot of reasons, so I shrug.

"Because we don't talk, Chase." He goes to the mirror to mess up his hair. "I swear to God, Gideon's better off than any of us, it's the truth. Because he doesn't have that . . . *drive* to communicate."

"Maybe he does. And just can't communicate it to us." I'm sick of talking about this, to be honest. But at least it's something to think about besides sex.

Noah takes a minute to catch his breath, then he says, "I can't stand feeling so goddamn responsible. I suck at this oldest brother shit. How did I get stuck with this?"

"We were born in the wrong order."

"I know. It's bullshit. I don't know how you put up with this as well as you do. Don't you ever want to be alone?"

"Not really."

"I don't even mean, like, physically alone. Just . . . don't you want to be able to make a decision without someone unnecessary complaining that they weren't consulted? Or stand in line at the grocery store without having to make small talk with the woman behind you? Or . . . I don't know, Jesus, take a shower without all the stupid things you said wrong the whole day bouncing around in your head?"

"You think too much."

"I know. I'm really, really aware that I think too much. Listen, Chase, this is the best advice I can give you. Don't ever let anyone tell you that college is for smart people. College eats smart people alive."

The restaurant is one of those steakhouses with dark wood booths and barely enough light to read the menu. When we go out, it's usually to a steakhouse; they tend to have macaroni and cheese, which is a staple when you have three kids under thirteen. But Claudia orders something in French, with a French accent, smiling the whole time at the short-haired waitress. Claude's wearing this dress—it's green and clings to her shoulders, and it makes me uncomfortable.

Gid tugs my sleeve when the waitress looks at him. **Want** he says, and points at a picture of a hamburger.

He completely couldn't eat more than two bites of that. It's about as big as he is.

The name's written right next to it—Southwestern Steak Burger. Maybe he'll pick at the bun. I look at his skinny little elbows. The boy needs to get more protein.

I point to a picture of a hot dog instead. Something he can actually manage.

No no no.

"Just a second," Claudia says, biting her lip at the waitress.

Dad says, "Just pick something out for him."

"He can choose his own food," Mom and Noah mumble together. They glance up at each other.

Gideon points to the hamburger.

Name tell me I sign.

He looks at the burger, looks at the name, looks at me. His lips pucker, and I wonder if he's understanding, for the first time, that there's a whole world out there that he's not getting, and it's more than just screaming parents and smoke alarms. I wonder if he ever thought that those strange symbols on paper have to do with our moving mouths he can't comprehend.

He's got to learn to read, but I realize I have no idea to what extent Gideon understands being deaf. Does he know that there are other people out there like him? Does he know this isn't going away?

I say, "He's going to have the Southwestern Steak Burger."

115

The waitress writes this down. "Okay, sure thing."

I look down. "Thank you."

Mom and Dad order wine—independently, by the glass, not the bottle. Mom orders red and Dad orders white, but they still take their sips at the same time.

"I'm not hungry," Noah complains to me, quietly.

"Are you sick?" He kind of looks like shit, and maybe that explains why he's been so weird lately.

"I dunno. Maybe."

For once, Gideon's not screaming and causing a scene, but Lucy's pounding her fists on her high chair and shrieking, so we're still getting stares. I want to apologize to everyone. To no one in particular, I say, "I'm sorry my parents think bringing a one-year-old to a restaurant is a good idea."

My mother sighs like Noah does. "Chase . . ."

Dad's laughing.

"And what's so funny?" she says.

"It's just that he's making this announcement to *no one* . . ."

Claudia gets up and goes to the bathroom. Dad's still giggling. "Oh, no, we've offended Claudia."

I snort, Dad catches my eye, and the two of us lose it. We're crying into our iced teas.

Mom says, "I . . . really don't understand what's so funny."

Noah says, "*I was assailed by memories of a life that wasn't mine anymore, but one in which I'd found the simplest and most lasting joys.*"

I gasp in air. "That's it. That's it exactly."

Dad leans on the table, shaking his head. "You guys are bizarre," he says, and I'm laughing even harder.

Gideon rests his head against my arm, and I lean down and kiss the top of his head. He's not laughing, but I still am, so he's shaking when I'm shaking.

My dad's getting a hold of himself. "You boys have a Camus quote for every occasion."

Noah and I look at each other. "It's more like ten Camus quotes that work for all occasions," he says, because I'm still laughing.

This is when Gideon reaches for another roll and spills his soda all over my shirt.

I completely fall apart laughing. I'm totally freezing. Ice sticks to my good tie.

"God." Mom hides her forehead in her hand. "God, I can't believe Noah is our most well-behaved."

Noah giggles. "I am the oldest and wisest, after all." He uses his cloth napkin to dab up the mess Gideon made. Gideon looks like he's about to cry, so I give him a hug and sign **fine**.

Sorry.

Sad no. I hug him again.

"Go clean yourself up," Mom tells me.

I head toward the bathroom, holding my shirt a few inches away from me, signifying to the other diners that this is not my fault. That this isn't my shirt or my mess. My life is just something that happened to me.

Of course, they probably just think I'm a psycho because I cannot. Stop. Laughing.

In the hallway outside the bathrooms, I run into Claudia making out with our waitress.

This is somehow not enough to make me stop laughing. I don't know. Maybe it's the shock. Or maybe I'm going insane from my virginity.

Claudia pulls away and smirks at me. "Oh, Chase, I'm so sorry!" she says, all her weight on one leg in a baby-slut pose. "I didn't think anyone would see us!"

This is hilarious. "Yes, you did!"

The waitress looks like she'd rather be anywhere else in the world, but I guess she should have thought of that before kissing a twelve-year-old.

This is ridiculous. I want to say, *Claudia, you're doing this so I will see you! You're doing this weird creepy sexy thing because for some reason you want me to look . . . just so you can say that I did.*

I say, "Look at my shirt."

Claudia stares at me.

I laugh. "I have *got* to do something about my shirt. I mean, look at you. You look so pretty."

"Chase, aren't you mad?"

I'm not old enough to be mad.

I roll my eyes. "At least *you're* kissing someone." I go into the bathroom and dab at my shirt with wet paper towels. I see myself in the mirror and smile and sign **fine**.

TEN

Still, after thinking about it for a few days, I decide it's a big problem that my little sister's getting more action than I am. I guess I could try something with Joanna, but she's started gushing about this tall surfer guy that comes in every day and buys Swedish fish from her. Like, seriously, how many Swedish fish does a guy need? One day he's going to come in and he's just going to have turned into a Swedish fish. She'll probably still want him. Damn it.

The only place to reliably find girls is downtown, at night, near the arcade and the ice-cream store, but I'm getting sick of downtown after wasting all my time here every day for work. After a few weeks of this, all the teenagers and their cars look the same. But, to be honest, slumming in the sand with my siblings isn't giving me the satisfaction I need either. I can't believe how long this summer's seemed. To quote Camus, *"At the other end of the city summer is already offering us, by way of contrast, its other riches: I mean its silence and its boredom."* We're here for only a few more weeks, and I hate that a part of me is looking forward to going back home. I should feel a lot sicker than I do every time I see a commercial for a back-to-school sale.

I sit on the beach after dinner and watch the waves. I wish some mermaids would pop out of them and take me away.

It hurts even more because I know the relief I need is a hundred percent obtainable, and is a hundred percent summer-approved. Melinda. Melinda Melinda Melinda.

And the satisfaction she offers is getting harder and harder to avoid, since it rains nearly every day for a week, and whenever it rains, Noah runs, sometimes for a few hours, sometimes for a day and a half. Leaving me here. Alone. Tempted. I feel like wherever I go, she's there. Unloading groceries from her car when I'm unloading from Mom's. Strolling past the Candy Kitchen while I'm on my lunch break. Strutting down the beach while I'm bobbing in the waves.

I need Noah to come home and prove to me that she's not as alone as she seems.

"Where the hell does he go?" Claudia says.

"Exercise," I say.

She goes, "Uh-huh."

When he is here, he does spend most of his time with Melinda—eating ice cream with her out on their porch, taking walks on the beach in hoodies and sneakers or ponchos, sometimes. They look stupid, like tourists who don't think to get out of the rain. This sounds so creepy, but sometimes I watch them in the evenings, just when they're saying goodbye. She'll be wearing some article of his clothing, and they'll be outside in the rain, her mouth absolutely nude in the rain, pouting toward him, quivering for more Noah, *stay stay stay*, Noah smiling like she's joking while he gives her a steaming kiss good night.

Fuck my window that sees straight into her bedroom. Fuck that Bella's not even in there with her to distract me. To bring me back where I'm supposed to be.

Every night, Noah comes back into our room, yawns, and pulls down the blinds without even glancing toward Melinda across the street where she's undressing or reading or crying. Then he tells me some stupid joke.

"What's brown and sticky?" he says.

I say, "What?"

"A stick." And he looks at me like I'm the weird one when I don't laugh.

He sleeps like the dead.

I sleep like a virgin.

Noah's happier than I've seen him in months. So I'd be an awful brother to get in the way of that. It's not like I have some relationship with Melinda. It was just a kiss. Am I going to ruin Noah's happiness because of a kiss?

I don't even know if I have the power to ruin it. How do I know if Melinda just wants to fuck with me, or if she actually wants to . . . fuck me? God, I don't know.

My life might be a cesspool of suck, but the rainstorm does stop eventually, so the beach becomes a part of our reality again. At least I have Shannon, and at least I have Claudia. Inexplicably, she and I have gotten closer since her stupid waitress-kissing incident—one that, she assures me, was just an experiment, what's the big deal, Chase, Jesus—and not close in a creepy incestuous way either, but in the way I assume guys are supposed to feel about their sisters. But what do I know? Clearly I don't get how normal people relate to each other.

Our new closeness is probably her doing, because after a while I notice she's making an effort to get along better with everyone. She's buying my parents newspapers when she goes out, cleaning up after Lucy, and at least making attempts at conversation with Noah, whenever he's around. It's like she thinks that if she grabs at everyone enough, we'll start copying and grab back. And they tell me *I'm* the clingy one. Noah and Claudia are probably worse than I am, when it's all said and done. They're just quiet about it.

Claudia starts joining me on the beach in the evenings. While Melinda and Noah are tackling each other into the spray, Melinda's legs long in her bikini, kick kick kicking, we walk together, far enough from the ocean that only the biggest waves lick our feet.

Most evenings, Melinda will suddenly push away from Noah at some point and put her arms around herself. She gives Noah small, angry looks, and he doesn't ask what's wrong. He never does. He touches her hair until she calms down. If she doesn't, he bails, and she stands by herself and stares out at the sea, wiping her cheeks now and then.

Sometimes Shannon comes out and puts his arm around her. He and Noah are both so much bigger than Melinda. For some reason I can't even begin to picture how I would look next to her.

"Stop *staring*," Claudia says. "Stalker."

I take my eyes away from Shannon's bicep.

Claudia pulls her hair back in her hand. "We could go break them up if you want. Dance provocatively in front of them or something."

"Claudia."

"You must miss Bella."

I exhale. "Melinda kissed me."

She tries to do one of those long, low whistles, but it sputters and hisses in her teeth.

I say, "Don't tell Noah, okay?"

"Yeah, I won't." She adds, because she's Saint Claudia, I guess, "But I'm surprised you haven't."

"I know."

"Be careful, Chase, okay?"

"She didn't hold me at gunpoint or anything."

"I know, just . . ." She watches Shannon and Melinda for a minute. "Just don't get yourself in a place where you give too much of a shit about . . . romance. We're only here a few more weeks, you know? You don't want to fuck up stuff with Noah just for some girl."

"I know that."

"Good," she says, and then she takes off down the beach to leap on top of Shannon and tackle him into the ocean. While they're shrieking, Melinda catches my eye. I'm about to open my mouth to say . . . God, who the hell knows, but Gideon ruins it or saves me by running up to me and screaming at me with his hands—**Mom ice cream now now now tell Claudia run run Chase chocolate ice cream whipped cream**.

Part of Claudia's peace mission included ending her moratorium on teaching Gideon new signs. She bribes him with cookies to get him to sit down with her every day and learn some new words. He picks it up a lot more quickly than any of us would expect, which is awesome. The downside is that she's now fully behind sending him to Deaf school. Deaf with a capital *D*, which means you're part of the Deaf community. And I'm sure that's awesome, but I don't think anyone but me understands how inaccessible that world is to us, and I can't believe how willing they are to surrender our seven-year-old to somewhere we can't follow him.

Claudia and Mom are chattering about it like it's a vacation we're planning. They're talking about all the research they've done and all the programs they think would be perfect for Gideon.

"It'll be good for him," Claudia says. She licks chocolate sauce off her sand-coated hands. "Think of how much ASL he'll pick up."

I say, "It's *residential* school. We'll never see him." I say, **Gideon napkin** but he's too busy freaking out about ice cream. You'd think we never feed the kid with how fucking excited he gets.

"We'll see him," Mom says.

"Do you know what they do to boys in those residential schools?" I ask, because I've done my damn research and I'm not afraid of an ugly truth if it will help keep my brother safe.

Claudia says, "What?"

"Don't you worry about it." Mom gives me a look.

I say, "Haven't you read about—"

"Chase."

Claudia says, "I want to know!"

"No, you don't," I say. "That's the point."

Claudia turns to Mom, her eyes big. "Like what happened to Melinda?"

I say, "Wait, what?"

Mom says, "We're not discussing this in front of Gideon."

"Gideon's deaf . . ."

"And going away to school," Mom says. "Pass the whipped cream."

I don't pass it. I sit on the couch and read more Camus. I don't want to think about what I've read the older boys at Deaf schools do to the younger boys. I don't want to think about what I've read happens to pretty girls at college parties.

Camus.

The only problem with reading so much Camus is that it gives Melinda an excuse to linger when she drops by. I tell her Noah's not here, and she starts to go, but she never really does. She always stays, clinging to our doorway, asking me how I liked *The First Man* or *Helen's Exile*.

So I tell her, I loved it, I loved it, I loved all of it, and she smiles with that mouth and says, "Me too, Chase. Me too."

Sometimes she reaches out and touches the inside of my wrist, and it feels like electricity.

"Have you told Noah?" she asks me one morning.

I say, "Told Noah what?"

She grins. "Right."

Exactly what is she worried—or hoping—that I'll tell him? That she kissed me? That I pulled away? That it took me a second to pull away?

So I say, "No."

"Huh. And I thought you two were close."

Later, Noah says, "You've been so quiet lately."

"I'm doing a lot of reading."

"I hear that's dangerous. Want a hug or something?"

I shake my head.

I'll be sixteen soon, and I feel like this summer has slipped by, in a lot of ways, despite its excruciating longevity. Dad's all anxious because the town hall is talking about building a dune in front of our house to stop all the sand from eroding away, and that means there'll be a long beach between our house and the water. None of us are excited about toting Lucy down there every day, every year, until she's big enough to make the walk on her own. I can smell the Coppertone Kids now.

"Oh, well," Dad says, whenever he gets too depressed about it. "You can't predict how anything will turn out, really. Stuff could be totally different next year." He smiles like a fisherman after a year of no fish.

Time passes so slowly. I work, I get paid, I have nothing to do with my money. Shannon buries himself in college books whenever he's not at work. This is ridiculous.

It's one of these nights that I can't sleep. I'm wandering around the upstairs, trying to convince Claudia to go to bed. "It's past midnight," I tell her. "Go to sleep."

"What about you?"

"I hate sleeping in the empty room," I explain. "I just need to wait until he comes back."

It's been two days.

Claudia sits in the hallway, knees tucked up to her chest. Mom and Dad and Gideon and Lucy are all asleep. Wherever

Noah is, he might be asleep too. Melinda might be asleep. It might just be us. Alone in the whole world.

I lean my head back until I hit the wall. My cheek rests against one of the knots in the wood. I can smell the cedar—actually, I have no idea what kind of wood this is, but my mind for some reason jumps to cedar.

The ocean sounds like a stomach growling. I wonder if we'll even be able to hear it when—if—they put in the dune.

She says, "What if he's not coming back?"

Melinda asked me this same thing this morning, when she came by to whisper in my ear, "*Many, in fact, feign love of life to avoid love itself.*"

"Leave me alone," I'd said. "I don't even know what that means."

But, come on, it's Camus, and I know what it means, especially now that it's two in the morning and I have no one but my little sister, and it's getting really, really hard to pretend that this is the life I'm in love with.

"He'll come back," I say.

And I'll just wait. Forever. I'll wait, and wait, and wait. And no one will care because they never expected me to do anything else.

Claudia says, "Yeah. I guess."

"Go to sleep. You're a growing girl or something."

She rolls her eyes. "I'll sleep if you promise you will soon too, okay?"

"I will. I just need a little time."

"Going to read?"

"Yeah, I think so."

But I don't read. Camus only makes me think of Melinda. He only makes me want to look across the street and see the light on in Melinda's room, see her sitting on her bed with that book in her lap and is she reading Camus? Does she love it love it love it? Does her house smell like cedar, and can she hear the ocean, and does she feel this . . .

. . . uselessness?

I walk downstairs for a glass of water, but I forget to be quiet. As soon as I've walked past his door, Gideon starts screaming.

No one in the world can scream like Gideon.

"Shit, shut up!" I rush into his room and say **Quiet quiet Lucy wake up**.

He's crying so hard. His breath is coming in these strangled little gasps like his chest is packed in ice. I go to his bed and hold him, pushing his face into my T-shirt. Noah's old T-shirt.

He grips me so tight, but I know, I know that he wants to talk, and one of the things I hate most about Gideon's fucked-up ears is that he can't hug me and talk at the same time. He has to let me comfort him before he can really tell me what's wrong. I feel his need to tell me, even though I know exactly what I've done wrong. I moved from where he thought I was. And he woke up to the vibrations that told him one of us was not where he'd trusted us to be.

Eventually he lets go, shaking while he does, and signs, **Late you sleep know no sleep you sick.**

Sick no sick no I sign, and squeeze him.

You here need you.

And my heart just breaks all over Gideon's bed.

Always. Always always. I spin my finger in so many circles. **I here you need me.**

Every once in a while I'll get these hints of what it means to be Gideon. I mean, I always think, *Oh, poor Gideon, he doesn't know what the rest of us are talking about,* but it's not all the time that I realize this isn't the sad part. It's not that it's sad he can't follow us. It is, but that's not the issue. The real problem is that Gideon lives in a world where the only thing he can count on is that we'll be asleep when we say we'll be asleep.

It's hitting me now, that I am not at all where anyone needs me to be right now. Gideon. Noah. Bella. Anyone.

OK. I sign. **My boy sleep.**

My boy sleep he says, and shows me the handshape for **I love you**, and I show it back, and sign **same** between the two of us. Literally, this means we're equal.

I squeeze him and tuck him into his bed, kiss his sweaty little forehead. I rub his back until he falls asleep. No one loves back rubs like Gid.

I should go to bed. He's trusting me. But I can't. I feel like I can barely move, and that means I have to, right now. If I lie down, all my muscles are going to atrophy and I'm going to curl up like a bug in the sun. I can't let that happen.

I can't just stay in bed alone because someone thinks that's where I'm supposed to be. I can't stagnate this entire summer away, not for anyone. Even if it's Gideon. He's going to have to trust me on this one.

I feel like I should bring a coat with me, but it's eighty degrees outside and I'm only going across the street. I don't even get to wait and angst at the doorway, Noah style, because Melinda opens the door as I'm walking up the steps.

I've seen him come up here a million times, but she always makes him wait. I've seen her watching him from the door of her kitchen.

"H-hi," I say.

"H-hi." She laughs. "Saw you on your way over. Here to discuss another essay?"

"Not exactly." I scuffle my feet. "Noah's not here, anyway?"

"Apparently he's in Rehobeth with friends. Thrilling for him, I'm sure."

That sounds right. I can see Noah there in my head, crashing on someone's couch, listening to the same ocean, just a few miles away. "Where are your parents?"

"Asleep."

"And Shannon?"

"Asleep."

Wow. Everyone is where they're supposed to be.

Including . . . Melinda pulls me into the house, into her room, into her bed . . . including us.

"What do you want from me?" I whisper.

I realize that I might know some things about sex, but I have no idea in what order everything is supposed to happen. When do the clothes come off? What do I touch first? When do I find out what happens when the kissing stops?

She says, "Shh."

My back is against her mattress. The last time I was in here, she told me about Camus. And Bella's stuff was on the bottom bunk.

Now, there's no one on bottom but me.

I say, "I'm just me."

"You *just* taste delicious." She works her lips down my cheek onto my neck onto my chest. She's running her hands up up up my torso, lifting Noah's shirt over my head.

"I don't understand," I say.

"There is nothing to understand. There is you and me and now."

"There's Noah."

"There's no Noah. Shh. You know he wouldn't even mind, Chase. He'd let us play."

But this doesn't make me any more relieved, just more confused. Would he mind? Probably not, but should he mind? Should *I* mind?

Noah is supposed to hate unproductive fun. And how is this at all close to productive? Melinda and I aren't in a relationship. We never will be. We're just having sex. I know we're going to have sex. I can feel it, and if I knew what it tasted like, I would taste it, but I don't know what happens afterward. I don't know who I'm going to be. Am I going to turn into Noah now?

Noah would let us play like two kids in a sandbox, because he would know that nothing would come of this. He'd know that once it's over, we'll both come back to him, just like we're supposed to, like coming home after school.

They should have named me Stay.

But I don't want to be good old reliable Chase tonight. I don't want to be the safe choice. Tonight, I want to be an asshole. I want to be Noah.

I try to kiss her harder, and she laughs. "What are you doing?"

"Going faster . . ."

She kisses me, slowly. I don't want her mouth on mine. I don't want to hold her hand. It's not like Bella. I want to close my eyes and have sex with her. I want this itch to be scratched, not tenderly kissed away.

I say, "Will it hurt?"

She laughs. "Um, shouldn't, not for you." She pulls off my jeans, then her voice softens. "Chase, you're shaking."

"I know, I—"

"Hey. Hey. Do you want to do this?"

"Please stop talking." I close my eyes. "Please, can we stop talking?"

She hesitates, then takes me in her mouth.

I can't speak and my mind is purple. I am so sweaty and her sheets smell like sunscreen and I'm so sticky and so fuzzy and coated in Melinda. I wonder if she'll protect me from the sun. I wonder if she'll protect me.

It's so hot that our bodies have to stick together.

"Here we go," she says, and she climbs on top of me. "Ready?"

I want to tell her not to speak, want to say it, but her lips are on mine again and I taste me and I taste her and I don't taste what we're saying and I don't taste Noah. I taste Camus—*I owe to such evenings the idea I have of innocence.*

ELEVEN

Wake up, baby Chase."

Oh God Oh God Oh God Oh God—no it can't be her I came back I'm in my room my house my world—

I open my eyes and see the ceiling fan slicing through the air. The same ceiling fan I once stared at when I was eight and had food poisoning and couldn't move. While I was puking, I imagined those blades cutting off my head, and they seemed like the only real thing in the world.

I'm in my room.

"Up, you, come on."

Breathe, Chase. It's Noah.

I sit up and wrap my arms around his neck.

It's bright and noisy outside, where the day-trippers are unloading their vans and hauling their three-year-olds out to the ocean. I can't believe I slept this long. Usually I'm up early, helping Dad with breakfast, getting the kids into bathing suits and sunscreen, yelling at Claudia to grab the umbrella as she leads the march out to the beach. Then Noah will wake up, finally, and we'll build a sand castle, or go for a run, and Mom and Dad will eventually drift out with their paperbacks and magazines.

I don't have time for that now. I have work in a few hours. But I don't feel like going in and smiling at Joanna or watching the surfer boy smile at her. I just want to sit here with my arms around my big brother. I want to build a sand castle with him, I want him to hold me, I want to run away with him and never move from right here.

"Um, hello there." He gives me a little pat on the back. "I just wanted to let you know that Dad's making waffles, so if you want a little sustenance with your antipsychotics . . ."

I let go and flop back against my pillows.

"You okay?" he says. "Gid was signing . . . something about you."

Yes. Gideon is tattling on me for being awake after

139

Gid-approved hours. This is so my biggest problem right now.

"I think I'm emotionally traumatized," I say.

"You'll fit in well with the rest of us." He fixes his hair in the mirror.

"I had sex with Melinda."

His face freezes in the mirror, then it slowly melts into his characteristic smirk. He turns around, leans against the dresser, and crosses his arms over his chest. *"Well."*

"I'm sorry. You weren't around."

"You're apologizing to me?"

"Yeah . . ."

He half-cough half-laughs into his fist, then studies me. "Are you okay?"

I squint. "What?"

"You're fifteen."

"Practically sixteen. And how old were you your first time?"

"Uh, eighteen."

"Jesus, Noah, seriously?"

"Last summer. Melinda was my first. And only."

I feel suddenly even worse than before, which I hadn't thought was possible, but Noah's just scrubbing at his hair and laughing. "Man, at this rate, we better pick up some condoms for Gideon." He raises an eyebrow. "You *did* use a condom, yeah?"

"Not exactly."

He throws a pillow at me.

"I, um, really don't think there was much pregnancy risk, given—"

"You failed to uphold your duties as a time-sensitive male? Aw, a little impatient?"

"Shitdamn, you don't have to shout it. I—"

He laughs. "Okay, okay, I don't need details."

But a second later, while I'm getting dressed, he says, "Did she do that thing with her tongue?"

"Which thing?"

He darts his tongue back and forth like a lizard.

God, I can still practically feel her down there. . . . "Oh, my God, yes! I thought there were aliens on me."

Noah laughs. "Yeah, and sometimes she gets a little too far *back*—"

"Ugghhhh." I cover my face with my hands.

"And then you still have to kiss her. . . ." He laughs. "Don't wear that shirt, man. That shirt is so old. Here." He tosses me one of his. One of his new ones.

I feel initiated.

"This doesn't freak you out, though?" I say. "Brothers sharing a girl? This is like the eighteen hundreds."

"Uh, yeah, Chase, this is the eighteen hundreds. Please,

we would have married Claudia off and mercy-killed Gideon by now."

Hmm.

He claps my shoulder. "Bros before hos, little boy."

I grab my cell phone and hit record. "Can you say that again? I want proof that someone *actually just said that*."

He smiles and sticks out his tongue, makes a face for the camera. Then he gets serious and moves his hand from my shoulder to the top of my head. "Just be careful, okay? I know that she's kind of . . . addictive. You have to know when to say no."

"Yeah." I stop recording.

"And I don't want to get in bed with her when you're in it." He shivers. "Ew." He hoists me onto his back and brings me down the stairs. I kick my feet against his hands.

Claudia says, "Happy birthday, Chase!"

Noah drops me and we both stare at each other and laugh. So *that's* why there're waffles!

Gid keeps signing **happy birthday** over and over even though no one's really watching him. But I appreciate it anyway. He signs really over the top, bringing his hands way away from his chest before he brings them back for **happy**.

Mom's feeding Lucy sliced-up strawberries. "You forgot your birthday, Chase? You really must be getting old."

"It's a little trickier when no one else is getting born." I kiss the top of Lucy's head. "Happy birthday, baby. This time last year we were burning turkey for you."

"We're going out to dinner to celebrate," Dad says, his voice all frank and resigned. I can practically hear the *shit-damn*.

Claudia goes, "Oh, God, no!"

Mom laughs. "Nowhere fancy, all right? Just out for some seafood. Somewhere we can get Lucy some people to scream at and Chase some crab cakes, all right?"

"All right." I look at Claude. "We're trapping you in the booth this time. There will be no sidling out."

"Please, who do you think I'm going to find at a seafood restaurant?" She slips a piece of a burned waffle into her mouth and crunches. She makes some dirty joke I can't quite make out around the waffle. Something about crabs.

Mom says, "What?"

"Nothing," we say together. I tuck Claudia under my arm, and we squeeze close. I say, "Can we bring Shannon? I've barely seen him outside of work in, like, years."

Noah walks over to Dad at the waffle iron and steals a fingerful of batter.

Mom says, "Just Shannon? That sounds . . . honey, let's keep it family. Or invite Melinda, too, at least."

Noah looks at me, eyes huge, finger in mouth.

"Family," we say together. "Family."

Claudia looks between us. "Wha . . . ?"

I pull her even closer. "Nothing!"

The doorbell rings, thank God. I shove Claudia away and walk backward down to the door to answer it, making faces at her as I go.

It's Melinda. She's wearing this pale yellow halter top. I never really understood halter tops until right now. Her shoulders are brown and boney. She snaps a bubble with her gum.

"Happy birthday," she says. She hands me this blue balloon. It's full of air, not helium, so it bobs instead of really floating.

I don't know what to say. I'm surprised she remembered. I say, "I'll share the balloon with Luce."

She smiles. "I had fun last night."

Over my shoulder, Noah clears his throat, and I feel his hand on the back of my neck. I'm really surprised by how tall he is. Then I realize he's actually standing on the step behind me. I like the effect, though. He feels like a giant.

She smiles, not really at him, but so obviously because of him. "Oh, hi."

"Come on, Melinda." His voice is soft. "What do you think you're doing with him? He's a kid."

Is he upset with her? But he wasn't upset with me. I don't understand. We did the same things. Am I really being excused—practically fucking congratulated—because I'm a few years younger?

Now there's quiet. She's scuffling her flip-flop against our walkway, jamming her polished toes into the wood, and I realize—she's embarrassed.

Did she think I wouldn't tell Noah? Did she think there was nothing weird about sleeping with a guy more than four years younger than her?

God, maybe she knew I would tell him. Maybe she wanted us to fight over her like hungry animals. I want to tell her that I can tell when I'm being used, but this seems like a lofty statement when I don't think I've ever been used before.

Oh. I'm being excused because I'm his brother.

Melinda gets ahold of herself quickly, raking her fingernails through her hair, rubbing her cheeks, telling us, *"To be sure, this cannot last. But what can last, after all?"*

Behind me, Mom and Dad are bitching softly to each other about something. I want to make Melinda watch. I want to tell her that this is what comes of relationships that weren't meant to be.

She waves good-bye and lopes back to her house, flip-flops kicking up little wisps of sand.

Noah closes the door behind her and raises his eyebrows at me. "Can you think of a more fitting quote?"

"Oh, I so, so want to."

"I *know*. Come on, we can do this. We've got to be able to outquote her. . . ."

I search for a second. "Um . . . Sisyphus! '*Yet at the same moment, blind and desperate, he realizes that the only bond linking him to the world is the cool hand of a girl.*'"

Noah offers me his fist. "*Very* nice."

I tap it with mine.

"What are you boys doing over there?" Claudia calls over the arguing.

Noah jerks his head. "Come on."

We step back into the kitchen. I smile at them all, even pissed-off Mom and Dad. "Melinda brought me a balloon!"

TWELVE

Dinner has barely started, and my father's already thrown back four shots of Jack Daniel's. And my mother is sucking on her third glass of red wine. Why are my birthdays always weird?

I have my elbow on Claude's arm so she totally can't move, and I'm way across the table from Gideon so I don't end up with soda on my shirt. Basically, I'm all set, as long as my parents don't get wrecked. Noah looks like he's crossing his fingers.

Lucy's screaming, but none of the surrounding tables are

complaining. This is our night, and they know it. They heard the waitress exclaim when she learned we had not one, but two birthdays tonight. "Twins?" she said, laughing.

I definitely pinched Claudia when she smiled at the waitress for too long.

The atmosphere must be getting to Gideon, because he's really talkative tonight. He reaches across the table to grab my hand and signs **today TV** and then stops. He has a face he makes when he doesn't know what he's trying to say; he pulls his lips in like this somehow keeps him from talking while he thinks.

I say, **What?**

He frowns, then picks up the crayons the hostess gave him. He still looks like he's five, so people give him shit like that all the time. He starts drawing on his kid's menu. It's clearly, obviously an octopus. Damn, that kid has talent!

I say, "Guys, Gideon can draw."

Claudia leans over and looks. "Way to go, Gid."

Gideon shows the picture to me.

"Octopus," I say, and take his crayon to write the name next to it in big block letters. He looks at it and nods. Not like it means shit to him. I can tell by the way he's clenching his fists that he wants the sign. That's such a rare thing. Maybe Claudia really is helping him.

I say, "Claude, do you know the sign for octopus?"

God, she doesn't, and she's beating herself up for it too. She bites her lips just like Gid does. **Animal eight legs** she signs to him.

He nods, hard.

Understand I sign, and he nods, makes a face that looks more like Noah than him, and picks his crayon back up. He's left-handed; all the brunets are. Figures they'd be the artists. I look at Claudia and Dad, my fellow blonds. What do we do? We dream while they do.

I put my head on Claudia's and mingle our hair. "We're so outnumbered," I say, and I smile at Dad, but he's drinking and studying this painting on the wall. Maybe he'll ask if it's for sale. He does that sometimes, though he never has any intention of buying. It embarrasses Mom.

"Hmm?" Claude says.

"The hair."

"We should have a battle," Noah says, marching two of Gideon's French fries across his plate. "Blonds against brunets." Gideon pokes one of the fries and Noah wiggles it at him.

Claudia laughs. "We'd destroy you."

Noah's eyebrows go up. "Oh, yes?"

"Please," I say. "We have Claudia. We're unbeatable."

Claude says, "And you're pretty damn crafty yourself, Chase."

Noah says, "Come on! I have *Lucy*."

"Pssh." Claudia waves her hand. "Lucy's a liability. Not to mention Gideon."

We all watch Gideon draw for a while. The crayon slips out of his hand, and he watches it roll away toward our parents. He signs **no** but doesn't reach for it, just pouts. Mom and Dad are too busy whispering to each other to listen to us fantasy fight, so I give Gideon back his crayon.

Lucy bangs on the tray of her high chair.

"You can't even talk to Gideon," Claudia says. "How would you share battle plans?"

Noah frowns. "Hey, I can talk to him well enough." He taps Gideon on the shoulder and holds up **I love you.** Gideon smiles and does it back, just like we did last night. "There you go," Noah says.

I say, "You could always get Mom to translate."

Noah glances at her, the same way we glanced at Lucy during the first few months every time we said her name or dropped a plate on the ground. To see if she was listening. Unlike Lucy, we get nothing out of Mom. Noah shrugs at me a little bit.

To nobody, I say, "I'm sorry Lucy's birthdays keep being so weird."

Claudia smiles.

Noah gobbles one of the French fries he's been playing with and stuffs the other one in Gideon's mouth. Gideon sticks his potatoey tongue out at Noah. Noah does it back. He says, "Well, you have Dad on your team, that's something."

I laugh. "Yeah, Dad can be tricky."

"Yes, he can," Mom says, quietly.

There's this lull, and I become very aware of the conversations at the other tables. Someone laughs at the next booth, throaty and fake. *Ha ha ha.*

Claudia says, "Mom?"

Noah glances at Gideon and says, "We're doing this now?"

"Yes, we're doing this now. That's enough." Dad plunks his glass on the table. "Katie?"

She shakes her head.

And no one says anything.

Ha ha ha.

I'm getting this terrible awful feeling deep in my stomach where nothing but my crab cake is supposed to be. Claudia's hand on mine is not helping. I really hope I don't throw up before I find out what the hell is going on.

Mom is still shaking her head, with this look on her face like she doesn't know what will happen if she stops and she doesn't want to find out. "We're not doing this now."

Noah slams his knife on the table. Gideon jumps, staring at Noah's face.

"Just say it!" Noah says. "Fucking say it already!"

Dad says, "Noah, you watch your mouth!"

"Will you folks be having any dessert tonight?" the waitress asks. Where the hell did she come from?

Probably one of us says *no, thank* you—probably Claude—but it feels like we just stare at her until she goes away.

Dad takes this shaky breath, then he turns and gives me this little smile. "You're right, Katie. All right. It's Chase and Lucy's birthday, okay? Let's forget about this and—"

Noah says, "And, what? Not talk? *Not talk?* No! Say it. We all know it, okay, so just say it!"

I can't figure out why Claudia's not holding my hand anymore, then I see her translating for Gideon, who's watching her hands like they're better than a million octopuses.

I wish she'd stop. He doesn't need to hear this.

Mom and Dad look at each other and my whole chest is going *pleasenopleasenopleaseGodno.*

"We're getting a divorce, guys," Dad says.

All my dinner's hanging out between my stomach and my throat, and every single one of my siblings looks the same, even Lucy, even Claudia. And I know, by Noah's face, that even though he knew it, he didn't believe it, even though we *all* knew it, we were all holding on, somehow, hoping they'd keep trying, that they could just keep on living and fighting. We trusted them to do that.

"No," Claudia says. "Just keep trying, okay? Don't give up, what the hell. This isn't like a do-it-yourself project gone wrong or . . . or a game of spider solitaire." She signs **spider.** "You wouldn't let us give up on *marriage.* This will get better."

"Just like, give it another go," Noah says. "Until we're all in college, at least. Do some goddamn couples therapy. Try actually working out what's wrong, for God's sake. Maybe it's good you got this out in the open. . . ."

I nod. "You hear all the time about people staying together for the kids. That could be you guys!"

Mom puts her hand on her forehead, and her voice is all pinched and whiny and awful. "We did that for nineteen years, Chase."

"No, no, come on, please," I say.

"It's Chase's birthday," says Claudia. "And Lucy . . ."

I whisper, "Lucy doesn't know what's going on."

Family together us together.

"We'll make it better!" Claudia says. "What do we need to do? I'll keep my clothes on."

I say, "I'll . . . tie up Lucy and make her stop crying."

Gideon signs **hear** and Noah and I are the only ones who see, and we completely drop everything and stare at each other for a second, our lips barely open.

Dad laughs, a little. "Come on, guys. Don't act like you didn't see this coming."

I can't even believe how gross Gideon's leftover French fries look. He's ripping one up with his hands, not looking at anyone, or at Claudia's translation anymore.

In the booth next to us, someone's laughing, and I'm suddenly aware that we're surrounded by families. These families that are chatting and laughing, *ha ha ha*, the ones that looked at us and smiled and were jealous of our two birthdays. These families are all around us. They're not a myth.

Families that talk.

Noah whispers, "No one's asked about who's going where."

I say, "What?"

"Custody."

Custody.

This is a word for other people.

Holding up my head is no longer an option. I sink down and put my forehead next to my stupid plate, and Claudia's hand is in my hair, she's going, "Shh, shh . . ."

Dad says, "We didn't want you all to have to travel back and forth. I'm going to get a place in the city, and with school . . ."

"You can't split us up," Noah says. "We don't do that shit."

Dad raises his eyebrows. "This coming from you?"

Mom says, "Noah, baby."

"I'm in college!" he says. "I can come home wherever I want, you guys can't change that! You can't tell me where to go!"

"Noah, shut up!" my father says.

Noah does.

And now we all fit the pieces together.

Dad hates Noah.

Lucy needs to be with Mom.

Dad doesn't know sign language.

I'm my father's favorite, Claudia would never live somewhere without me. . . .

And so there it is. We've already been divided. We've been divided the same way for years. Blonds against brunets.

I look up at Noah, and he's looking at me, too. He breathes out very slowly.

At some point, the waitress brings Lucy and me these little matching chocolate cakes, and Luce totally annihilates hers with her baby fists. I give her mine, too, and we watch her keep smashing.

Melinda answers the door with a book in her hand.

I say, "Shut up," before she can say anything, and I kiss her with every bit of anything in me.

We roll around like animals in horrible, horrible heat. I barely get out of her bed for three days.

THIRTEEN

When we're almost done packing up the car to go home, Shannon comes and sits on the towel next to me. I'm throwing clods of sand down toward the ocean. But I'm so far away that they're just smashing on the beach, like tiny, worthless bombs.

It's three days post-birthday. They should all three go down in the awkward hall of fame. There's nothing worse than two rival teams in one house. Eating together, watching TV together, sunbathing together. Washing their socks and underwear and team uniforms together. Unwilling unwilling

unwilling to cut the trip short "just because of what happened at dinner."

No wonder I spent most of my time hidden away in
Melinda's room.

"So you're going home now?" he says.

"Yeah." I'm not sure why he's asking this. It's pretty obvious. I turn toward the house and look at everyone hauling suitcases and shit to the car. "As soon as everyone's packed up."

"Uh, what home are you going to?"

"There's only one home, Shannon." I stop throwing and
pull my knees up. "My dad's going to get his own place soon
enough. And Claude and I will live there."

"Like, same city as your mom?"

"Yeah, I think so. So I won't have to switch schools. So
theoretically I should see them still, except . . . except Noah
will be at college, and Gid's going away to Deaf school, so it'll
just be Mom and the baby."

"What about summers?"

"I don't know."

"But you'll—"

"Hey." I turn to him and stick my hand in his hair. "I'll be
here. Next summer. I'm coming back here. Okay?" I dig my
feet into the sand. "*Nothing* could stop me from coming here.
Nothing."

He nods, squeezes my hand for a second, then he shoves me off of him. "Okay."

"Chase?"

I turn around. It's Mom. I totally feel like I don't have to listen to her anymore. That might turn out to be a problem. Maybe not.

She says, "Could you please find your brother?"

"Which one?"

She sighs, like I ask this question just to annoy her. "Noah."

"Okay. I'll see what I can do." I stand up and give Shannon a hug. "I'll see you next summer, man. Send my love to Bella."

"Um, Melinda wanted to—"

I'm totally gone before he can finish that sentence. Though I'm not going to lie, a part of me wonders what else Melinda wanted to do. What else is there to do?

Noah went over last night to say good-bye to her. That's enough for all of us, I think.

I walk down the beach for a while. I'm pretty sure I'll eventually run into Noah. I saw him less than an hour ago. He couldn't have gone far.

And there he is. He's down where there are no more houses, throwing sand into the ocean just like I was. Except he's close enough to the water that his throws actually make it in.

And I'm pretty sure that he's crying.

I say, "Noah?"

He breathes hard. "Say good-bye to your fucking beach, Chase."

I put my hands in my pockets to stop me from putting them on him. It's not the time yet, and I know it, but that doesn't stop me from instinctually wanting to touch him. Claudia's been trying to train me not to be too affectionate, but I don't know how well it's working.

I say, "We'll be back, man."

"We'll be back in fucking pieces! We'll be back with a huge fucking dune on our beach, Chase!" His arm whirlwinds, scattering sand everywhere. "Fuck this fuck this fuck this fuck—"

I can't take it anymore. I stand behind him and put my arms around his waist.

He stiffens immediately, then relaxes his weight back into me. I feel his backbone against my chest. He heaves.

I hear the ocean and my brother crying and that's it.

"We will come back here," I tell him. "All of us. I promise."

"Won't be the same."

"Dude," I say, letting go. "Camus. It's *'ever the same sky throughout the years.'*"

Noah wipes his nose. "'*I live in my family, which thinks it rules over rich and hideous cities built of stones and mists.*'"

I give him a little smile. "That'll do."

He says, "Chase . . ." and draws circles in the sand with his foot, concentric ones, smaller and smaller and smaller until he can't draw them anymore. He says, "I wish we were together. So much. You know that, right?"

I nod.

He holds out an **I love you** and says, "Stay absurd."

I show it back and say, "Stay happy," because the concepts are supposed to be linked. They're supposed to both be possible. Different, but maybe a little bit the same.

He might not be a great brother, but he's always been one to me.

Back at the house, I hug stupid Mom and blabbermouth Gideon and sleeping Lucy; I hug them extra hard and prepare for the long ride home and the longer wait for next summer. When we will come back.

17TH SUMMER

FOURTEEN

A day comes when, thanks to rigidity, nothing causes wonder any more, everything is known, and life is spent in beginning over again. These are the days of exile, of desiccated life, of dead souls. To come alive again, one needs a special grace, self-forgetfulness, or a homeland."

This is the quote playing in my head. I know a lot of the longer ones by heart now. Ones that aren't even in *The Stranger.* Camus has kept me sane through the winter.

I'm driving. Dad and Claudia are both asleep. Claudia's just plain worn-out—being thirteen is apparently some kind of hard work that I've forgotten—but Dad's sleep is all passive-aggressive protest. He and Mom still don't appreciate us kids "going behind their backs" and planning our beach trip together.

Claudia was pretty dumbfounded the first time she heard this. "You heard us on the phone to Noah," she said. "You heard us *all year* on the phone to Noah promising we'd go together."

"You kids." Dad made that expression he's made a lot since the divorce. Like we're stabbing him with knives, but we're too cute for him to fight off.

I said, "Come on, Dad. It's our place."

"All seven of us in the house together? That doesn't sound hopelessly awkward?"

Claudia, always the sensitive one, said, "No, it sounds hopelessly awkward for *two* of you. The rest of us still love each other, despite the separate houses. Asshole."

Dad had sighed, gathered her under his arm, kissed the top of her head. "What am I going to do with you?"

"Come to the beach with us," she'd said, in her newly honed you're-an-idiot voice. He agreed. Since Mom did, as well, I assume a similar conversation happened over there. Without the snotty teenage girl.

Despite what a raging hormonal bitch she's been lately,

I really do love Claudia and I'm incredibly glad she's around. I still don't have a girlfriend, so she's the only female influence in my life, and I guess it says something that she hasn't made me dread the sight of anything with boobs. All I see of Mom and Lucy are Christmas card pictures and the odd weekend here and there. I babysit and bring Lucy to the park sometimes. I only ever see Noah and Gid when they're out of school, first of all—Noah doesn't commute from home anymore—and then out of Mom's grip.

I'm also glad Claudia's around to have conversations like that one with Dad. She says all the shit I'm still too nervous to say. In spite of her bloodline, Claudia's managed to hold on to the part of her that says things. I know Noah's proud.

"She knows this trip is something we need to do," he said during our last phone call. The reception is shitty in his dorm, and it always sounds like he's a million miles away.

"It is like spitting in Dad's face, though."

Noah said, "'*Every rebellion implies some kind of unity.*'"

I turn onto our street and note the Hathaways' empty driveway. Maybe they're not coming this year, or maybe they came and left early. I'm sort of hoping. I mean, I'll miss Shannon, but it's probably for the best. The hellos are harder than the good-byes. Every year it gets more and more awkward. Harder to pretend we're still the same kids who ran on the beach together.

I'm trying to pretend Melinda has nothing to do with these thoughts, because I've spent the whole year pretending Melinda has nothing to do with me. It's tradition now.

I see Mom's van in the driveway, and my chest feels full at the thought of seeing my family, and then I notice the beach and it all comes crashing into my stomach.

I knew they put the dune in, but I heard it from Dad, so I'd thought about it, like he did, in terms of property values and sightlines. I didn't think about the fact that this place no longer looks like my beach.

There's what looks like miles and miles of sand between the house and the ocean. We used to be able to run from our front door to the water without running out of breath. Now it's a genuine hike. Now you'd have to bring a cooler if you wanted to keep your drinks cold.

"Guys," I say.

They have the same light-sleeping gene as Gideon, except they respond to noise. They crack their eyes open. Dad says, "Shitdamn, look at this."

Claudia lights up and bounces. "That's the van! They're here!"

"Yeah, Claude, but look at the beach." I pull into the driveway.

Claudia's quiet for a minute. "Ah well. Still the same beach."

I love that Claudia, the one who always scoffs at our Camus habit, is the first one to reach this revelation. Maybe she really lives the philosophy as much as the rest of us. She just doesn't know it. Noah would think of some clever analogy relating existentialism and deafness, but I can't shake out the wording. Something about whether it's better to know or to not know that you have no idea what you're doing.

Camus keeps me sane.

I don't even stop at the house; I head straight out to the sand. My goal is to see how long it takes to get to the ocean, but two minutes in I see Noah and stop keeping track.

I run up to him and he hugs me, that big warm hug with two arms and slaps on the back. "Hey," he says. "Welcome home."

"Backatcha." I haven't seen him in months, and even though I talk to him every day on the phone, it's not the same. We've shared so many details of our day-to-day lives that finding something new to talk about feels almost impossible. We should say something important, but there are too many excuses not to have to speak—Claudia, the sand, the sun. I'm not sure quite how to start. "How was the drive up?"

He waves his hand. "Just fine. Mom did most of it. Hey, Claudia!" He picks her up and twirls her around, and she laughs but clings on to me as soon as he puts her down. Noah makes this big show out of not noticing.

"Are the kids inside?" I say. I realize I expect Gideon and Lucy to be together, despite the age difference, the same way I always expected Claudia to be with Gideon.

Noah rubs his hair. "Nah, they split when Mom started unloading and tried to commandeer us into helping." He points to the water. "I'm keeping an eye on them."

And there they are, my two youngest siblings, wrestling in the sand, splashing each other with water from the breakers. Lucy's shrieking, and Gideon's making that same haunted laugh. I'd worry that he was going to hurt her, if he weren't still almost as small as she is. And Lucy's a good swimmer, even for a kid who's a few weeks shy of two years old. I used to take her to lessons sometimes when Mom was working. She kicks with the best of them.

"Gideon's just not growing," I say.

"Yeah, but he's a cutie. Have you seen him lately?"

"Not since Christmas."

Noah blows air out of his mouth. "Wait until you see him sign."

"Oh, yeah?"

"See for yourself."

I trudge down to the waterline. They're on their bellies, gripping the sand and shrieking as the ocean pulls them in and pushes them back out.

I say, "Hey, guys!"

"Chase!" Lucy jumps up and wraps her wet little self around my legs. Her water wings squish against the back of my knees. I reach down and tickle Gideon's foot so he'll notice I'm here, and his face opens up.

Chase! he says, then starts signing stuff I completely don't know.

I sign, **slow slow slow, OK.**

OK. He throws his arms around me and smiles when he lets go. He's still got that baby-smile, even if he's clearly no longer a baby. **Nice see you.**

Nice see you same. Short still.

I know I know. Little brother me.

"Come on," I say, talking and signing simultaneously for the first time in what feels like years. "Let's go see Mom, okay?"

"'Kay!" Lucy says, dancing ahead of me with those flat-footed toddler steps.

Hate Mom Gid signs.

I don't have the willpower to sign **lie** to this anymore.

They both get tired before we're even close to the house. It's probably less than a hundred steps, but I feel a million pounds heavier from the sun, even more so when I scoop up my tired siblings and haul them the rest of the way. When I finally reach the house—Gideon on one hip, Lucy on the other—Mom's already out in the sand. It's weird to see her out here; I just assumed the beach wouldn't be her thing anymore. She looks happier to be here than Dad did. She has a glass of lemonade and a smile, and she offers them both to me.

"Here," I say. "Take a baby." She takes Lucy, and I kiss both their cheeks.

"You happy to be back?" she asks me.

I nod. "You and Dad will be okay, right?"

"Chase, of course. It's only a few weeks. And we'd do anything for you kids."

Except keep us together, but it's been a year, and I can't be too resentful about this anymore. It's just how it worked out. We aren't a cohesive family anymore; we just aren't. And it sucks, but I can deal. I can love Gideon and Lucy, even if they aren't mine anymore, and . . . and Noah was never anyone's to begin with.

I hand my lemonade back to Mom so I can sign **Noah where** to Gideon. He points down the beach. Noah's running around with two big dogs—they got *dogs*? When did this happen? I went to pick up Lucy three weeks ago. . . .

Noah grabs the dogs by their collars and spins them in tight circles, calming them down, then brings them back to us. "Dog!" Lucy cries, and wraps her arms around her neck.

Noah catches my eye, and I kick myself for being so stupid. I know whose dogs those are.

I crane my neck and look across the street. There's Bella, dragging a suitcase out of the SUV, arguing with Shannon. She's nearly unrecognizable, with all her hair chopped off and her ballerina body even longer and leaner.

And there's Melinda. And she looks exactly the same.

She gives me this wave. My stomach hurts.

I don't think Noah's seen Melinda since last summer, though I know they've talked, but she was off traveling Europe or something, while Noah was in class learning Spanish and French and Italian. He doesn't look particularly happy to see her. I'm imagining European men with their hands all over her, and I wonder if he is too.

Noah sighs. "And," he says, *"'one always finds one's burden again.'"*

It's the same beach, but I feel so cold, even though it's

July and I'm still sweaty from the hike from the ocean. And I have Gideon in my arms, his head on my shoulder, and Claudia clinging to my arm like the rest of our family is made of strangers. You know, I want to tell her, it's ever the same family throughout the years. But Noah would think I'm talking about the Hathaways, and I'd probably hurt Mom's feelings just because she doesn't understand, and Lucy would notice her shaking chin, and Gideon would stick his thumb in his mouth and close his eyes so he wouldn't have to listen.

Shannon has it in his head that he has to go to Dartmouth or his life will just explode. Applications aren't due for another six months and he's already freaking out about essay topics and whether he should appear focused or open-minded in his list of after-school activites.

"Where are you applying?" he asks me. We're in his room. He used to have all these posters in here of models in tiny bikinis. Now he has posters for cars and bands I've never heard of. The lead singers are all skinny with stringy hair.

"I have no idea."

"You should start thinking about it. Your whole life is where you went to college."

Except my life is the part of the year when you're not in

school, but I couldn't stand it if he rolled his eyes to this. So I don't say anything. I say, "What about Melinda?"

Shannon looks down. "She'll go back to college someday. Whatever. She will."

Bella comes by Shannon's room to ask if a shirt is hers or his. She gives me a polite smile. "Hey, Chase. How've you been?"

"Fine. You?"

She nods.

Shannon says to me, "I have a college book you can borrow, if you want. And I can show you around the common application, let you see how it's done."

Down the hall, I hear Melinda and Noah, laughing.

"I should get going," I say.

We figure restaurants are just a bad idea, and Noah and I convince Mom and Dad that we really, really don't want to spend our first night here with the Hathaways, so it's a family dinner at home tonight. I can't say I'm surprised that Noah needs a break from Melinda. He was there for three hours, and that was longer than I was ever able to go without feeling a little suicidal.

We order in a few pizzas and sit around our big dining room table, letting the kids keep stuff from getting too awkward. It's noisy and rowdy and reminds me of when I was a little kid and our cousins used to come over. And you remember which cousins you like the best, and which ones they like the best. And you know you're not supposed to be awkward with them, that they're family, but sometimes the comfort is forced. Blood can only stretch so far, I guess.

But right now, Gideon's drawing us together, because we're all pretty fascinated with the signs he's learned since he went to school. **Sign favorite show** I say.

He pauses for a second, then makes a fist with one hand and snatches at it with the other.

We all sign **what, Gideon?**

He signs, **game good fight good**, then he shrugs and fingerspells **w-i-n.**

Noah can't quit smiling at him. For the first time, we're all making real efforts to sign every time we talk, to do our best to translate every bit of the conversation for him. Because he cares now. He's got this air about him now, like he deserves to understand conversations. Like he thinks the things we talk about are important.

Noah looks at me for a second and mouths, *Oh, he'll learn.* I smile. Gideon signs **what what**, thinking we actually spoke.

"What we really need," Dad says, looking out the window toward the ocean way, way out there. "Is an extension on the balcony. Just build it a few more feet out toward the water. We don't even need new supports for a few extra feet."

Mom takes a bite of her pizza. She and Dad are sitting across from each other, a few seats down the table from the rest of us, letting the kids—and me and Noah—handle the signing and the yelling and the pushing and the shoving. They're acting like civilized, friendly people, just like they did on Thanksgiving and Christmas and whenever we all had to be together, and I love them. I really do. They could have made this so much worse.

Mom says, "I can get someone out here to look at it."

"Aw, what fun is that? Chase and I could do it, right?"

I glance at Noah, then my father. *It's not that he hates you*, I want to tell my brother. *It's not that anymore. It's that he's used to me being his oldest—his only—son.*

It does sound kind of fun. "Yeah, Dad, sure. We'll do that."

He smiles.

Noah looks at me. "So. I've been reading Camus—"

Everyone groans but me and Gideon. Even Lucy joins in, with a big smile on her face, echoing Mom's tone as closely as she can.

"Camus?" I make my eyes wide. *"No way!"*

"In French," Noah says.

Claudia says, "You know French?"

175

"I took, like, all language classes this year. I am going to be a man of the world someday. But French is my worst. I'm only getting like every other sentence."

"You're just not very smart," Claudia says seriously. Dad smacks her on the back of the head.

Noah ignores all this and talks right to me. "It's brutal. It's . . . you hear about Camus being so much better in French, and—"

"And I know. We're never going to get it." I've thought about this before, and it kills me. That one of the most beautiful parts of my life isn't nearly as beautiful as it's supposed to be.

I think of Melinda, for some reason, and I wonder if she still wears the same perfume. She always smelled like candy canes. . . .

Read Camus Gideon says, then points to himself.

We all turn on him, our mouths saying, "Shit, Gideon, *what?*" but our hands just saying **really?**

He nods and signs something I don't get. I see **school** and **book** but—

I turn to Claudia. "What was that?" and I'm acutely aware that Noah picked it up, that Noah is currently signing to Gideon and I can't. Living with Gideon—even though I never picture them together, since they're always off at school—must have given him the edge. The odd weekend here and there. The bullshit holidays. Those times must make the difference.

"They got to pick books in school," she says. "Easy books. *The Stranger* is easy."

"Easy to read, not to understand." But I don't care that Gideon is eight, that he's still learning to read, that he's probably missing everything important; I care that, for the first time, I have something I can share with both my brothers.

I'm completely smiley and teary and happysad.

"Who's next?" My mom laughs. "Lucy?"

"No." Noah smiles across the table. "Claudia."

Claudia snorts into her pepperoni. "I'm not reading your goddamn Camus. I live in the real world, thanks."

Noah says, *"'There is but one world, however!'"*

She rolls her eyes.

I say, *"'A world that be explained even with bad reasons is a familiar world, but, on the other hand, in a universe suddenly divested of illusions and lights, man feels an alien, a stranger.'* Umm . . . *'His exile is without remedy since he is deprived of the memory of a lost home or the hope of a promised land.'"*

They all sort of stare at me. Claudia gave up trying to translate in the middle, but Gideon's smiling at me anyway.

"What?" I say. "I like my Camus."

"Boys are fucking obsessed," Claudia mumbles.

"Hiding behind an attitude is no better than hiding behind literature," Noah says patiently.

Gideon finishes his pizza slice and looks at our parents. They're talking together, quietly. I watch him decide to disturb them, change his mind, and turn to sign **more pizza please** to me. I stand up and go to grab him a slice, and all their voices swell behind me as Claudia starts a new story and everyone laughs, even Lucy, even Gideon.

Claudia once told me that story about Beethoven. The time he wasn't facing the audience after a concert and had no idea the people were cheering. And so his clarinet player or something came and turned him around, and he saw it all for the first time.

I turn around now, and see them laughing, but unlike Beethoven, I could already hear them. I always knew they were there. Behind me. Even this whole year, when I didn't see them, I always knew they were there.

The lack of surprise doesn't make it any less awesome. Because I get a different revelation now, better than Beethoven's. I'm in love, not with Melinda or Bella or the girl from my physics class or Joanna from Candy Kitchen, but with my stupid, fallen-apart family.

*　　*　　*

Noah doesn't get home from screwing Melinda until about two, and he immediately goes out to the balcony. I sneak outside.

"Hey." I hand him a spoon. "Brought ice cream."

He exhales. "You're a saint," he says, and we dig into the carton together, looking far far far where you can still just barely see the edge of the sea. I think this is some kind of soy nonfat ice cream Mom got. I've missed this. I'd started to take it for granted that ice cream tastes good.

Still, I can only eat so much before I give up and lean against the railing, strumming my guitar.

"So how'd it go?" I ask.

He licks his spoon. "She cried when I told her I wasn't spending the night. I hate when she cries."

"Me too." But she's only cried with me once. It was during that weird three-day marathon sex-spree between my birthday last year and the day we left. Or the day before we left, more accurately, since I eventually couldn't stand to look at her any longer. I'm still trying to forget. I'm still trying not to think about the way she smells.

"And she talked about you," he says.

"God, she *always* talks about you when I'm with her. *'Noah kisses me softer than that.'*"

"*'Chase is so much more passionate.'*"

"*'Noah takes his time.'*" I play a minor chord.

179

"'*Chase doesn't hesitate like you do.*'" Noah digs an almond out of the ice cream and tosses it off the balcony. "God. Why do we come back to this girl, Chase?"

I lean against the railing. "It's part of the summer."

"Yeah, sure. Sno-balls, sand castles, breakers, and Melinda. Year after year after year after year." He sighs. "Man. When do you think this will stop?"

"What will? Melinda?"

"Nah, not Melinda. All of it. Defining our lives here, calling it home, even though we spend eleven twelfths of our lives somewhere else."

"The somewhere else changes, though. You spend most of that away at school. I spend it in a home that isn't the one I grew up in. This doesn't change."

He says, "The dune . . ."

"Fuck the dune. It's the same beach."

"Yeah."

"So maybe as long as we come here, this will be home." This will be our constant.

He's quiet. "When do you think we'll stop coming here?"

"I guess when we grow up."

"God, I'm twenty years old, Chase." He messes with his hair. "You're almost seventeen. This whole growing-up thing, when does it happen?"

"Not for a long time, hopefully."

He laughs. "You're always the same. What's that that Melinda calls you?"

"Chase Everboy McGill." Another minor chord.

He's still laughing. "Yeaaaah."

"Okay, but what's wrong with that, per se? Where is it written that we have to grow up?"

"I think J. M. Barrie wrote that."

I laugh a little. "No disrespect to Mr. Barrie—"

"—I think he might be Sir Barrie."

"If he's not, he should be." I do love *Peter Pan*, and I love the story behind it even more. "But . . . J. M. Barrie is not Camus."

"What if we had chosen J. M. Barrie instead?"

"To be our guide?"

He whistles a few bars of that song from *Pinocchio*. I try to play along, but he's going too fast.

"Yeah," he says.

"One of us would have died in an ice-skating accident. How old was Barrie's brother when he died? Eight?"

"Something like that."

"No ice-skating accidents for us, though." I set down my guitar. I can't concentrate. "That's a winter thing."

"Uh-huh."

"And we're Camus boys."

"God, why did we even choose Camus?"

It feels sacrilegious to even ask. "I don't know. Because that's how it worked out, I guess. And we can't get out now. Stuck here forever and ever. Stuck in the summer."

Noah sighs and looks out over the sand. "*I learn that there is no superhuman happiness, no eternity outside the sweep of days.*"

"Days and days and days," I say.

Noah looks down. I wonder if he's sore. "And days. And days."

FIFTEEN

I don't go out to the beach much in the first week we're here. There's nothing to do out there. Shannon is working or studying all the time, Bella's asleep whenever she's on the beach. Noah's always over at Melinda's, fucking or fighting, and Claudia never wakes up before two. So I just hide in the house for a few days, waiting, dreading, hoping for the day Melinda eventually seeks me out because she's tired of Noah or tired of not pissing him off enough.

It's not like I'm hard to find. But so far, she hasn't come.

On Tuesday, Dad makes me take the car to the hardware

store and pick up some shit for our project. The roads seem slower and dustier than before—I guess that's the effect of driving on your own. I'm not used to it, not even at home, where Claudia tags along even if I'm just running to the drugstore. Now she's too busy working on her tan.

I'm lugging the boards and hammers I bought back into the house, sweat pouring into my shirt collar, when Melinda shows up and stands on my driveway, sucking on a Popsicle.

"Can I help you?" I say.

She shrugs. Her toenails are painted lime green.

"Want to give me a hand?" I say, definitely not expecting her to say yes.

She doesn't, just licks a drop of syrup running down her hand. "You haven't been over yet."

"No."

She sways back and forth, making those awful sucking noises. Only Melinda could remind you of sex by acting incredibly unsexy. "Noah's been over practically every day."

"I've been busy."

"Doing what?'

"Babysitting."

"Noah doesn't babysit?"

I snort. "No."

Boards, saws, nails, screwdrivers. I wish I hadn't bought so much stuff. I wish I had Noah-muscles and I could carry this all in one trip. Or maybe Noah himself or my other worthless brother could come out here and help me. Or, hey? Dad? Finish what you started?

I look at Melinda. He'd just tell me the same thing.

I wonder where you're supposed to draw the line. When am I allowed to give up? Give up on hauling construction tools in one trip. Don't give up on a marriage. Don't give up on your brother. Give up on Melinda? *Line in the sand* is such an appropriate cliché.

She says, "Noah's not as good as you."

"You tell him the same thing about me."

"Oh, come on, Chase." She drops her Popsicle on the ground and takes my sweaty shirt between two of her fingers, like it doesn't weigh anything. Like I don't weigh anything, and she can just close her eyes and wish for me to go somewhere and I'll go.

I pull away.

"You're Noah's," I say.

Her face squishes into a ball. "I'm not *anyone's*."

She's making her rape victim face. I don't how to react to that. It always makes me angry, just like when she cries. I know that's an astoundingly inappropriate response, but I can't help it. I always get the feeling like she expects me to apologize every time I say something that reminds her of it. Apologize for the rape, not for being mean.

And that makes me feel dirty. And meaner.

But being with her always does, so maybe I should be used to it.

I pick up another box. "I know what happened to you."

She looks so young and small and stupid in that green tank top. Why did I used to think she was an older woman? "When did Noah tell you?"

Really, it was Mom and Claudia who told me, that night we were talking about residential school. But Noah did tell me, eventually. He called me from his dorm room after a talk with her. He was almost crying, he was so frustrated.

I say, "Like, February, but it was nothing I hadn't already guessed."

"I didn't think you needed to be told, asshole. I sort of implied it pretty hard that time under your house, remember? That night your balls finally dropped?"

I throw the box in the sand. "Fuck you, Melinda."

"Aw, you're so sweaty. Let me get your shirt off."

Why, *why* do I let her take my shirt off?

"Mmm." She kisses my right pec. "The off-season was good to you." She crawls her lips over my neck, up my chin . . .

Anyone could see us. But I can't think of anyone who

would give a shit, besides the twins. Dad would probably think the whole situation is hilarious. Mom doesn't know what to do with me anymore. Gideon and Lucy wouldn't understand, and Claudia wouldn't be surprised. Noah would probably breathe a sigh of relief, or sympathy.

Melinda tastes like those cheap Popsicles I hate. "Mmm." She licks her lips and says, "You taste like Noah."

I try to turn away, but she's holding on.

"You can't leave me, Chase." She tilts her head. "I was your first. I'm your summer."

Oh, Goddamn.

I don't want her. My brain knows that I don't want her. That she's Melinda and, whether she's an older woman or not, she's old, and whether she's Noah's or not, she's sleeping with Noah, and whether she's my first or my last, she will never be mine.

It is always easy to be logical. It is nearly impossible to be logical to the bitter end.

In a second, I'm in her bed.

God, we're so hot and sweaty and I smell like nails and rust all over and she smells like fake sugar. Why do I always end up in this girl's bed? Why am I asking God for help when Camus says the universe is an apathetic place?

You know what's an apathetic place? This bed. It is

objective and unstoppable. It's impartial and it doesn't care if I'm here or Noah is here as long as someone is. I doubt anyone really gives a shit which one—me, Melinda, and Noah included.

"Oh, kiss me all *over*," she says, her head on my chest.

"Stop talking." I've told her before I hate it when she talks. I always feel someone else can hear us. Like we're being judged.

"Aww, Chasey." Her mouth is on my neck. "Keep yelling at me."

"I'm not yelling, Christ. This is not some weird sex tape." This is not a rape fantasy.

"It could be."

"Ewwww." I close my eyes and try to will this all to be gone. Her. This bed. My erection.

It's so easy to not want her when she's here. It's during the year, or when I see Noah walking over, that I pine like a fucking dog. And I do, as much as I hate hate hate to admit it. I write her name in my notebook, then furiously scribble over it, then write it again. I lie in the sand and think about her fingernails. I imagine her body when I'm in the shower. I hate myself for never appreciating her.

But when she's here, I just want her to be better than she ever is.

She's like Christmas. And I'm a summer boy.

I wonder how much longer until I come.

Back and forth back and forth back and forth day after day after day after day. . . . Is this still the same time? Was I just lugging boxes, or is this one of the millions of other times I've accidentally stumbled into this bunk bed? Is this really the first time this summer?

It's hard to breathe when there's a sticky girl on your chest.

Then the door opens.

"What? *Chase?*"

Oh, shit.

Bella is so far away from my life at this moment that I'd almost forgotten she exists.

My first thought is *Cover up Bella is beautiful and innocent and cannot see you like this.* Is she still a virgin? I think she'll always be a virgin even if she grows up and has like fifteen kids like the lady on TV.

My second thought is *Oh God, I hope Shannon's not here.*

Melinda picks her head off of me. "Oh, hey, Bella. Just fooling around."

"With *Chase?*" Bella's chin trembles. "No, this isn't right, this isn't how it—"

"I know!" I sit up and Melinda basically falls off of me.

And the bed. "I know! This isn't how it's supposed to work! I'm sorry." I say to no one, "I'm sorry no one understands how this is supposed to work. Even me. Even me. I'm sorry."

I stand up and start getting dressed. Bella's still standing by the door, making noises like she swallowed something alive.

I hope it's not my naked body that's shocking her this much.

Melinda says, "You'll be back. I know you will."

"No." I shake my head. "No, I've got to stop doing this, messing this up—"

"But you're so perfect."

I stare at her.

She's lying on her side, reaching out for me. She looks drunk, floundering around in the air. Like she's trying to find me, like she can't see that I'm right there.

She whispers, "*Whatever it may say, our era is deserting this world.*"

I push past Bella as gently as I can.

Melinda says, "Wait, your shirt—"

"Keep it," I say. "Keep it, God, it's Noah's."

What's weird is that nothing comes of it. Nobody explodes. My parents and Mr. and Mrs. Hathaway have no idea what's going on, or, if they do, they don't take the time to confront Noah and me about it. Noah and Melinda keep going exactly how they were. Bella completely ignores me, which doesn't feel very different from usual. As far as I know, Shannon's oblivious.

For a few days, it's like Melinda and I have never slept together. Every time I talk to her, all she wants to talk about is Noah, and not in the sneaky, sexy way she used to. She comes to me asking for relationship advice. I think she's trying to rub it in my face, then I realize that all her questions actually have more to do with Noah and me as brothers than her and Noah as . . . whatever they are. Maybe she's the one who's jealous.

I don't tell her that my entire relationship with Noah is me making up rules that he has, for some reason, decided to follow.

"Where does he go?" she asks me.

"Nowhere special. The going is the important part." I'm in the kitchen, scrubbing up the spills from the lunch I made for the kids. Now everyone except Lucy, who's fussy today and lying on the couch crying, is on the beach with Shannon. My parents are at couple's counseling—not getting back together, they keep telling us, though some part of us doesn't believe them—and Noah's run off somewhere. Everyone's where they're supposed to be. Except me and Melinda. And Bella. Wherever she is. I don't care as much as I probably should.

"The journey is the destination?" she says.

She should stick to quoting Camus. It's the only time she sounds smart. I say, "You're going to have a fun time with Noah if you get it into your head that you're supposed to keep track of him."

She leans over the counter. "God. God, Lucy's just screaming, isn't she?"

"Yeah, I don't know. She's been doing this all day."

"How old is she?"

"She's . . . two, she's really loud today. Luce! Quiet down, baby girl, okay?"

Melinda picks her head up and raises her eyebrows at me. "Has she been in the water a lot?"

"I mean—"

"Maybe it's her ears."

"Her *what*?" I say, kind of ironically, I guess.

Melinda goes to the couch and kneels beside screaming Lucy. "Lucy Lucy Lucy, can you sing something for me?" she says.

Lucy just ignores her, and I envy her ability to do so. Melinda examines her anyway, pulling Lucy's brown curls out of the way. "Christ, Chase, I knew it. Come look at her ears."

"Her ears are fine. Trust me. We've made pretty damn sure."

"Yeah, well, now they're red and infected."

"What? Nooo." I drop my sponge and basically leap over to the couch. Melinda shows me her ears, and God, she's right. . . . God, that must hurt like a *bitch*. . . .

"Shannon used to get them all the time when he was little," Melinda says.

"So did Gideon. But I can't remember what we did. . . ."

"Uh, antibiotics? And ear drops, probably. Where are your parents?"

"Remembering why they divorced each other." God, I wish Noah were here. I pick Lucy up and cradle her. "Okay, we'll borrow my dad's car, okay? We'll take her to the hospital—"

"There's a hospital here?"

"Where do you think she was born, Candy Kitchen?"

Lucy's car seat is at therapy with the parents, so Melinda holds her on her lap while I drive to the hospital. This is pretty thrilling for the little peanut, so she quiets down some, pressing her palms against the window.

I'm breathing way too fast. Melinda keeps telling me to slow down.

I know, logically, that Lucy's going to be fine. I mean, little kids get ear infections all the time. Gideon got so many that Noah used to suggest we just cut the things off. But one of the consequences of having so many siblings is I've never ever been alone when one of them was sick before. Not even last year. Claudia never gets sick.

And now my hand that isn't driving is clinging to Melinda's thigh like I think she's about to jump out of the car with my baby sister. The one who gets sick. The one I'm alone with right now, because Melinda doesn't count.

Everything will be ruined forever if I don't fix Lucy. We will miss her too much, and fall apart, and Mom will never trust me again, and Noah will know that he's been wrong all along, thinking that I was trustworthy enough to play oldest brother for him.

Lucy's still crying. Melinda bounces her carefully, says, "Shh."

"Can you go deaf from ear infections?" I ask.

Melinda says, "Chase—"

"Just answer the question."

She sighs. "I think, yeah, it's theoretically possible."

"Holy shit!"

"Yeah, Everboy, and it's theoretically possible I could go deaf from listening to you whine, all the time, that someone's gonna go deaf! Shitdamn!"

"God, don't say that. Never say that again."

"Shitdamn!" Did she get that from Noah? I've never heard Noah say shitdamn. Did she hear it from Dad? Or, God, from me? Did I give her that word?

The clinic is the ten longest miles of my life away from the house. I kill the motor in the closest parking spot and make Melinda give me Lucy so I can carry her inside. "You go get paperwork or something," I say, and I sit in a chair with Lucy. "Heyyyy, Luce. Stop crying, baby girl, okay?"

Her chin trembles.

"Say my name, Lucy. You know who I am?" I hold her close. "I have you. You're safe with me. I'm sorry sorry sorry."

Melinda sits down beside me with the forms and asks me questions, Lucy's middle name and native language, just like the forms at the speech therapist's. Without Noah to snark, everything's going quickly. I actually know the answers this time, until I realize, two questions late, that I gave my address and not Lucy's.

"Shit, go back, change that one. That's my dad's address."

She looks up. "I thought Lucy lived with your dad."

"No, I live with my dad. Lucy and Gideon and Noah live with Mom. Only Claudia and me with Dad."

"Oh, I—"

"You what?"

"I thought you lived with Noah."

God, how many times will she have to sleep with one of us before she understands that *nobody lives with Noah, Noah just sometimes lives with you.*

"He's not your boy," I say, quietly. "And he's not mine either."

She scratches her chin with the end of the pen and fixes the address.

The part where we actually see the doctor is pretty painless—especially for Lucy, who gets a big dose of children's Tylenol—but the waiting is brutal. All of it. Waiting for the nurse to call our name, waiting for the nurse to take her vitals, waiting for the nurse to get the doctor. Waiting to hand over my Dad's credit card to pay. We're standing in line at the pharmacy downstairs when I seriously can't handle it anymore. I hand Lucy to Melinda and head outside and try to breathe. Sea air and all that, but it's not helping.

I call Noah's cell phone. This is about as productive as calling Gideon.

"Noah, it's me," I tell his voice mail. "By the time you ever listen to this I'm sure you'll know all about Lucy's ear infection and she won't even have an ear infection and she'll probably be like seventeen and about to go to prom, but . . . but I'm scared and I want you to come home. I'm really really scared. You have to stop running away, man, I need you, and I'm going seriously crazy just here with *Melinda* so please come home, okay? Even if you get this message fifteen years from now. Stay home. Stop running."

"Feeling better?" Melinda is standing behind me, paper bag with Lucy's ear drops dangling from those stupid long fingernails. Luce has her head buried in Melinda's neck, and I wonder what she thinks of her perfume.

I don't say anything.

"I'll drive," she says.

"No." I get into the driver's seat.

She gets in, studying me. "I thought he wasn't your boy."

I stare at the dashboard. "I lied."

"Oh, yeah?" She pulls the seat belt over herself, over Lucy. "Why'd you do that?"

"Didn't want to share him."

I turn the key in the ignition.

"Well, that hardly seems fair." Melinda plays with Lucy's hair. "He always shared me."

I try to breathe slowly.

When we get home, Noah's in the kitchen, eating banana bread. I know by the weirded-out look on his face when I hug him that he definitely didn't get my message. But he's here and I'm here and Lucy can hear.

"Um, hi?" He pats my head, probably getting crumbs all in my hair. He holds out the pan to me. "Want some?"

I do, of course. I take what Noah offers and hope he'll offer himself.

But I'm not complaining. He already gives me more than he gives anyone. Even if he never answers his damn cell phone, he still calls every day.

SIXTEEN

Adding the extension to the balcony is pretty fun because it's my father and me twenty feet up in the air with a bunch of tools, and neither of us has a clue what he's doing. Every once in a while Noah or Mom will come out here, mutter something about we're going to kill ourselves, then disappear—literally, in Noah's case.

I sort of like that Mom cares about Dad the same way Noah cares about me.

"So she loves you, right?" I ask him, because I guess this is the simplest way to describe it.

"We were married for like twenty years, Chase," he says, hammering a nail where a nail completely doesn't need to be. "Love would be the obvious remainder."

"I thought you were supposed to hate each other after a divorce."

"I don't think there are any *supposed to*s with divorce besides *divorce isn't supposed to happen*."

"Insights from your couple's counselor?"

He laughs and saws off the end of a board. "No, the couple's counselor thinks divorce was the best possible solution for your mom and me. Though she does talk a lot about how hard it is on you guys." Dad looks at me. "So how hard is it on you guys?"

It's about four o'clock and wicked hot, and all my muscles hurt. Probably would have been smarter to wait until evening to deal with this, but after all these years with Gideon, we're used to doing loud things when they can be seen.

Melinda and I always had sex with the lights on.

I can hear the kids shrieking down on the beach.

"I mean . . ." I shrug. "I miss them, but Gideon's at Deaf school and Noah's at college and . . . I'll be at college in a year. So it's not like I would have seen them all the time anyway. This was sort of how it was going to be even if you stayed together."

"Hmm. I seem to recall asking a completely different question than the one you just answered."

I roll my eyes and laugh. "Yeah, it's hard and it sucks. I miss them all the time." I look down at them all running around in the sand, tackling one another, screaming in their distinct voices. I can tell each of them apart, and all of them apart from everyone else on the beach. "I miss them right now, goddamn it, and I'm *looking* at them."

Dad laughs. "You want to take a break? Go play with them?"

The problem is I'm sixteen, almost seventeen, and I don't want to play with them as much as I *want* to want to play with them. Maybe this feeling is what Noah's been running from.

God, he'd think that was a stupid thing to say.

"You don't have to be afraid of this growing-up thing," Dad says.

"Shit, inspirational speech?"

"Camus-boy, you're always going to be the same you, just older. It's not like there's a moment when you wake up and go, *Shit, I'm grown-up, I don't feel like myself anymore.*"

I don't tell him, but this is the scariest fucking thing I've ever heard in my life. Being grown-up *should* feel like a big transition. It can't be something that, despite my best efforts,

I've been drifting closer and closer to every summer. It needs to be a shock. I need to know at what point to stop holding on. And that moment will suck, and probably every moment after that will suck, but at least I'll know that everything that came before really was valid. I really was young and innocent. I wasn't fooling myself.

Down on the beach, Shannon scoops up Gideon and holds him over a breaking wave, and Gideon kicks and kicks and—

"Chase?"

I come back. "Sorry."

"Listen," he says. "We can talk about a new arrangement for next year. Maybe we need to rethink this. You could live with Mom for a little while, or go over to her house after school. Or Gideon could come stay with us for some of his breaks, or we could put you guys on rotation month by month or something, so you all get to live with each other for a while."

I shake my head, digging out the nail my dad just bent. "Claudia needs me."

He waves his hand. "Claudia will be fine. Claudia's always fine."

I look at him. "You need me."

He looks at me for a second, then pulls me into a hug,

screwdriver and all. "Oh, you." He kisses the top of my head. "Just wait until you wake up fifty-four and alone."

I'm playing guitar at night again. Why do I never play when I can see my fingers? I stretch my legs out in the sand.

"It's going to be just how we planned," Shannon says, holding Gideon on his lap. "I'll marry Claudia and you'll marry Bella and Noah will marry Melinda. Just like we always planned."

Oh, Shannon.

Gideon reaches out and touches my fret hand. It's too dark to translate to him but not too late for him to be awake. The guilty hour, basically. After eight years of this, though, he accepts it, and sits quietly, playing with the sand on either side of Shannon.

I just say, "Mmm."

Claudia's down by the water, alone, in that green bikini, just staring out over the sea. She's beginning to get a few curves, but mostly she's stick straight all the way down, just like Lucy or Gideon or something.

Shannon sings, "Gid-e-on," quietly, into the back of his head. "I'm going to miss him when he's too old to be held."

"I don't think he'll ever be too old to be held."

Gideon sifts sand through his fingers.

"God, I hate that I never get out here anymore," Shannon says. "Too busy with applications. Next summer, I think we should get jobs together. We should be lifeguards."

"That would be really cool, actually."

"Yeah, wouldn't that be awesome? We'd get to lie around on the beach all day with those big orange floats, have ladies coming and checking us out while we put on sunscreen? Yeaaah, that is the life, Chase. And then at night we could find some cool people and get drunk, or make a bonfire or something, or just cruise around downtown. . . ."

"All right. Next year."

"Next year."

Right now next year seems a million miles off. I feel like I finally get what Dad kept saying last summer: anything could happen between now and then. There's no way to tell where we'll be this time next year. Instead of making me nervous, the uncertainty is making me numb. How much can I care when I don't know how much will stay?

Gideon turns and signs to me, and I only get about half of it. **Again**, I say, squinting through the dark.

Sleep now you read me.

Yes. I take Gideon's hand and pull him off Shannon's lap. "I'm gonna put him to bed," I say. "I'll be back out in a second, okay? Don't let Claudia commit a dramatic suicide."

204

Inside, Mom and Dad are watching the news, Lucy snuggled between them on the couch. Mom starts to stand up when she sees sleepy Gideon, and I say, "No, no, I've got him. You're good." I'll let them stay.

I ask Gideon what he wants to read, and of course he signs **C-a-m-u-s**, so I run upstairs and get my book. Even though he's awake—even though he *knows* I'm awake—I'm terrified he's going to feel my footsteps and freak out. I keep shaking my head to clear it.

Reading to your deaf brother is weird, but Gideon and I have gotten used to it this summer. We have a routine. Basically, I sit with him squished into one side of me and trace the words with my finger and we read them together, and he puts his fingers over my lips and feels me say the words. It takes me a while with how slow I have to go with him, especially when I'm reading the essays. Not all Camus is as simple as *The Stranger.*

Gideon's still eight, though, so sometimes he'll get bored in the middle of an essay and randomly flip pages and point to a new place, and I'll just have to start wherever he points. It sort of makes my brain explode. Maybe someday we'll unlock the mystery of the universe this way. It's all a code when you read every eleventh word and skip nine pages, or something.

He points to a passage and I read. *"'His scorn of the*

gods, his hatred of death, and his passion for life won him that unspeakable penalty in which the whole being is exerted towards accomplishing nothing. That is the price that must be paid for the pass—'" I stop and clear my throat. *"'Passions of this earth.'"*

With his free hand, Gideon signs pieces of the words that he can translate from English to ASL, skips the ones he can't. Sometimes he fingerspells, but his school is training them out of that. **Speak ASL** he explained to me. **English no.**

He flips the page and points.

I glance ahead to see what I'm reading and feel my breath catch. I am so glad Gideon can't hear how shaky and awful my voice is. *"'But being pure is recovering that spiritual home where one can feel the world's relationship, where one's pulse-beats coincide with the violent throbbing of the two o'clock sun. It is well known that one's native land is always recognized at the moment of losing it.'"*

Melinda once read me that one.

I didn't understand it then. Back when I had a home.

I pretend to be smoothing his sheets so I get a second to collect myself. **OK.** I kiss the top of his head. **Good sleep.**

More?

No. Tomorrow.

I love you.

I love you same.

Every time I sign this, I wonder exactly what it is I'm saying. The same as what? The same as he loves me? No, I don't. The same as I love everyone else? No. I love him different, and I probably always will.

Even though I'm supposed to go back out to Shannon, I blow past my parents and Lucy on the couch and go out to the balcony, gulping down the air. Stars are totally pouring all around me, but I don't feel them. I don't feel much of anything, except hot.

It's the same balcony, I'm trying to tell myself. It's torn up and there're nails everywhere and I could probably pitch myself off the edge with little or no effort, but it's the same balcony. And the girl down by the water, holding hands with Shannon? That's Claudia. The same Claudia.

If everything is the same, why does it feel like everything's been ruined, and that I was the one who did the ruining?

Next year will be different. Next year has to be different. I sit down on the balcony. *For the first time, in that night alive with signs and stars, I opened myself to the gentle indifference of the world.*

"Be careful out there," Dad calls.

I just want to feel like me for the rest of my life. I cover my ears with my hands.

And not like this.

*   *   *

Claudia makes a funny face when she answers the phone. "Yeah, sure," she says. "He's right here." I think she was hoping it was Shannon. I'm not sure what's going on with them. I'm sort of afraid to ask. It looks very delicate.

I'm teaching Gideon a few chords on my guitar. Claudia taps me on the shoulder with the phone. "I'm hearing, you know?" I said. "You don't have to accost me."

Gideon holds his cheek against the guitar to feel the vibrations. Someday I'm going to have to tell him that Beethoven story.

"It's Melinda," Claudia says.

Fuck. "What does she want?"

"She didn't say. She's calling, like, all the time, isn't she?"

"She probably misses Noah."

"What do you have to do with her and Noah?"

"God, Claudia, I don't know." *It's not a lie.* "She's probably just going to ask me when he's coming home and I'll tell her I don't know and she'll whine at me and . . ." *We'll have sex.* "Entertain Gid for a minute, okay?"

I take the phone upstairs and close the door to my room before I lift it to my ear. "Hello?"

She's breathing like she's crying.

I should ask what's wrong.

I should be pissed off like usual. But I'm not, not this time.

I hope she doesn't say anything.

She doesn't.

I sit against the door and slide down, holding the phone to my ear. I breathe back.

For God knows how long, we sit there. Breathing.

SEVENTEEN

Everything gets better when Noah comes home. It always does. He's been gone so long that, instead of being mad, we've all looped back and are just happy to see him. Mom and Dad suggest we celebrate, and we order in pizza, because that's how we celebrate, clearly, now that restaurants are taboo. Not that anyone's said this out loud. Of course.

"Stop it, Chase," Noah says, because I'm looking at him like I think he's grown since the last time I've seen him. "It's been three days."

I wonder if he got my message, finally.

"I missed you," I say.

He laughs, serving pizza to the kids. "You know who really missed me?"

"Uh, Melinda. She's been chasing me ever since we took Luce to the hospital." I'm back to hating her. After all, I thought we were done. I gave her Noah's shirt and everything. Honestly, what does this girl want from me?

"Yes, indeed," he says. "Oh, she missed me, all right."

Claudia's picking through the mail—we get it diverted here, otherwise it'd be a fucking disaster by the time we get home—and she picks one letter out and pinches it between her fingers like it's one of Lucy's diapers. "Letter from college, No."

Noah plucks the letter from Claudia's hand and reads it leaning against the refrigerator, munching on a banana. He always eats fruit before he eats junk food, ever since he was a kid. It's like a deviation on a salad for a kid who can't be normal about anything.

I go over to check on Lucy, who's asleep on the couch. She's worn out with the fever that came with the ear infection. Gideon's getting lazy too, and even dizzier than usual, so we're checking his forehead a lot and keep looking at his ears, which completely baffles him. **Ears fine** he tells us. **Ears plastic.**

Mom and Dad are quipping over whose onions are pervading whose onion-free slice, but they're arguing like high schoolers doing that *Stooooop it, no you stoooop it* thing. It makes me happy and itchy all at the same time. I wonder if they're about to make out over the pizza, and I wonder how I would feel about that. I know I wouldn't feel comfortable eating it anymore. The pizza, I mean.

I go back to the counter and stand next to Claudia as she sifts through the mail. Her hair's all sweaty and she smells like Noah's banana. "There is *nothing* interesting in this mail."

"Shame," I say, and she elbows me. She's in a good mood because she and Shannon are now *going steady*. I honestly wonder what decade they're living in, but it's hard to be cynical when you remember that summers always feel about twenty years behind actual time, anyway. And I'm very proud of Shannon's ability to stay innocent in the end.

Noah stretches and finishes his banana. "Pizza." He gently moves Mom out of the way, kissing her temple. "Stop flirting with my father for a second, darling."

She rolls her eyes like Claudia does. "Oh, all right."

"What's the letter?" I ask.

He tosses it to me and drops a kiss on Gideon's head on his way past the table. "Schedule for next year."

There are so many acronyms on this page that it takes

me a minute to figure out that these are practically all ASL classes.

I fold the page halfway. "Noah?"

He smiles at me, at Mom and Dad, at all of us. "I'm going to be a sign language major."

My parents look like they've just discovered that the innocent-looking onions they were so playfully fighting over actually have a hidden agenda. Mom's eyebrows are all bunched together, and Dad looks about ten years younger, just like he always does when he's confused. Gideon's face with blond hair.

I say, "Noah, that's awesome!"

He smiles at me. "Figured my lack of knowledge is a problem I need to fix. Since Lucy's starting to sign better than I do."

This is an exaggeration. Lucy's only signs are **bad Gideon**, **I love you**, and **no**, which gives you a good summary of their relationship.

Still, I'm grinning all over the place. "Noah, that's awesome. That's *awesome*, Noah. You're totally going to have to teach me once you're fluent."

"I will absolutely."

Claudia mumbles, "College is stupid," and starts picking olives off her pizza. I think her disdain for Camus has extended to include all education.

"Noah," Mom says quietly, eventually. "Noah, what are you going to do for a job, sweetheart?"

He shrugs and takes a bite of his slice. "Whatever I need to do, I guess."

"No," Mom says. "What are you going to be able to do with a degree in sign language?"

"Talk to my little brother, hopefully." He looks down at the floor. "I've come to believe that that's important."

I wonder how Melinda would feel about this.

I think I'm proud.

My father says, "What kind of career—"

"Jesus Christ," Noah says. "If one more person tries to talk to me about a career, I'm going to fucking explode. Like having a career is some necessity, like it's the same as having a family. Like those are two things to *balance*." He shakes his head. "I could be an interpreter. Whatever."

Dad says, "Listen, Noah, we'll get you some tapes or something. Don't waste your college years on something you could learn from a few books, yeah?"

"Dad, what can you major in that you *can't* learn from a few books? What do you want me to major in? Engineering?" he points at Dad, then Mom. "Psychology? So I can do what, have five kids and divorce my wife?" He shakes his head. "I can do that just fine with a degree in sign language, thanks."

He looks to Claudia for support, but she's totally not looking at him, just flipping through the newspaper. She decided, somewhere between now and when she started *going steady* with Shannon, that she is anti-conflict. Or at least focused on *real* conflicts. She quotes statistics about people in Africa or Washington, D.C. like we quote *The Stranger* or *Return to Tipasa*.

Gideon stamps his foot so I'll look at him and rubs his fingers together like there's something between them—that easy sign for **what's going on?**

I try to catch him up and pay attention to Noah at the same time.

Dad says, "Noah, the way to prove your point isn't to be so fucking combative all the time—"

"Oh, should I just walk out, then?" Noah throws his pizza crust onto his plate. "Because I know how you love it when I do that."

I'm telling Gideon **Noah learn sign school** when Gideon gets all upset and starts signing **no no no** all over the place.

"We just want you to have a good future," Mom's saying.

"Oh, yeah, and I've really been prepared for that. Good thing you started giving a shit about my upbringing *now*."

"Goddamn it, Noah, show some respect!" Dad yells.

"I don't have any fucking respect!"

"Guys?" I jerk my thumb over to Gideon.

He's standing on his kitchen chair, throwing pizza crusts at Noah to try to make him turn around. He is also yelling in that tongueless voice of his.

He points at Noah with his whole arm. **Sign not school.**

Noah signs, **Help you.**

No. Sign life mine. Not yours.

For a minute Noah just stands there, and I see him melt. It's like everything he's ever done and hated—and there's a lot, you can see it in the way he bites his lip—is melting from the top of his head into a puddle on the floor, and now he has to stand in it.

I'm scared he's going to drown.

And he looks at me, and I see everything in his brain spinning around, everything in him realizing that he doesn't belong in this family, that he's the only one of us who needs classes to talk to Gideon, that all this time all of us, even him, have been wondering why the fuck he had to run all the time when the real answer is that we pushed him because he wasn't good enough and we did not have time to wait.

He doesn't fit in with any of us.

Expect for me.

Except for me, and that's why he's looking at me. And that's why he's walking to me and holding out his arm. And

I am going to him and gripping his shoulder because I need *something* to happen, the same way I needed something to happen last year, the first time I went to Melinda. I can't sit in this house anymore. I need a push, and I never thought I would be lucky enough to get it alongside this brother.

They just need an older brother. Noah needs *me*.

"Bye," I whisper, on our way out the door.

Running away is obviously Noah's area of expertise, so I try not to protest anything he does. Even when we leave without bringing the six-pack of Coke sitting on our steps, the one Gideon complained was **too heavy** and left there post–grocery shopping. Even when he stops at the Hathaways' house and picks up Melinda.

It's hard to keep quiet for this one. I'm okay with riding in the back. I'm not okay with who's now riding shotgun.

Melinda!

"So." She smoothes her dress over those *legs*. Why, why does this girl look like sex? I thought sex was supposed to be *awesome*.

Noah says, "We need to go buy some presents for Chase."

"Oh?"

"Tomorrow is his seventeenth birthday," Noah says.

Maybe it won't totally bite this year. But considering

I'm totally running away with Noah and *Melinda* the day before . . . I'm thinking it will.

He says, "Let's just go down to Dewey and get a motel for the night, okay? There's good shopping down there, and . . ." He sighs. "And Chase has to be back by tomorrow."

"You have to be back by tomorrow too," I say.

"Chase. I'm here. With you. I'll be with you tomorrow, with you for your birthday. What other reason do I have to go back?"

"Lucy?"

He groans. "She won't know if I miss it."

I remember every frickin' birthday that Noah has ever missed—eighth, ninth, twelfth, fifteenth—but I don't say anything. I'm still afraid that he's going to kick me out of his little journey, which is really stupid now that I know my presence is the only thing giving him permission to run away this time.

It's starting to rain. It's always weird when it rains here; the sand gets these impressions like big fingerprints.

In the front seat, Noah is explaining everything to Melinda. The sign-language major. What my parents said. What Gideon said.

Noah says, "The huge part of the world that Gideon will never get? There's about that much that I won't get about Gideon."

Before this year, before reading Camus with him, I never would have thought that there was that much about Gideon to understand. I had no idea Noah went through the same change of heart I did. I had no idea he knew the ability to speak with Gideon was worth any real sacrifice. I sort of thought I was the only one of us who knew that.

And until today, I thought Noah still thought talking was worthless.

Melinda's saying something along these same lines now, and I remember that she's the one who planted that concept in our heads in the first place. Just like all the other things she's planted in mine. Camus, sex, the idea of Noah as a white knight, the idea of night as something more frustrating than dangerous. She planted a lot of stuff, flowers and weeds, and all of it's growing now in the rain.

She might be awful, but at least she made me think.

What's that quote? Right—*Beginning to think is beginning to be undermined.*

I guess when you're having sex with someone five years younger than you, you have to undermine him any way you can.

This kind of perspective is making me feel old.

But Noah, up in the front seat . . . my brother is making *her* think, and older woman Melinda has never looked so small.

And I realize that I can love Noah to pieces, but I really don't want to be him when I grow up.

"Come on," he says. "That pizza was shitty. Let's get some food."

We stop at this diner where we used to get breakfast as kids. Noah stirs his coffee with his pinkie finger. Melinda and I both order strawberry French toast; Noah doesn't order anything, but he picks strawberries off of her plate and never mine. Melinda builds a tower out of nondairy creamers.

In the other booths, people are talking quietly, loudly, but all of them are talking. I scratch my wrist; restaurants still give me hives.

To nobody, I say, "I'm sorry the only things I can think to say are Camus quotes."

Noah smiles.

Melinda, her hair dripping onto the table and her eyes dripping shut, whispers, "Noah, you start."

He thinks for just a moment. "'*Unconscious, secret calls, invitations from all the faces, they are the necessary reverse and price of victory.*'"

I say, "'*In Paris it is possible to be homesick for space and a beating of wings.*'"

And I know by the look on Melinda's face that she has us both beat. She clears her throat. "'*Everything related to* death is either ridiculous or hateful here. The populace without religion and without idols dies alone after having lived in a crowd.'"

Noah and I are, of course, quiet.

Noah's takes his pinkie finger out and licks it. He says, to nobody—not to me because it's not true, not to Claudia and Lucy because they never needed him, not to Gideon because it wouldn't matter and he wouldn't hear—"I'm sorry for being a shitty older brother."

Melinda has the decency to stay off his shoulder, and I swallow it all with my strawberries.

We get two motel rooms—one for me, one for Noah and Melinda, though it'd be cheaper and more logical just to get one huge bed for all of us. Of course, none of us says this out loud, though I know we're all thinking it. Especially when Noah and I both retreat to my room to change, as if either of us has anything to hide from Melinda. It's like we're acting as ourselves in a play, but we forgot to read the character notes that say we all have sex and make each other uncomfortable, and that is our motivation for every single thing we do.

It's also stupid to have two rooms because we spend all our time in Noah and Melinda's. And we sleep. All of us on the floor, none of us in the bed, we sleep. Curled into distinct little balls. We forget whether we're conscious or not. At any given time, one of us is probably awake. But no more than one.

My time alone is just after two in the morning. I should check my cell phone.

Melinda is drooling on her arm, eyes twitching underneath their lids. Noah looks like he's in pain, but then again he always does when he sleeps.

I think I'll never fall asleep again, then I do.

The sun comes up. It makes no difference to us. It keeps raining. It's my birthday.

Here we are—it's sometime around six in the morning. There's wreckage from the minibar littering the floor and music from some ongoing party downstairs throbbing through the carpet. We're dirty and sweaty and sticky and fat and sad. Noah's sitting against the door like a hero ready to shoot an intruder, or maybe the intruder himself keeping us all hostage. Melinda's hanging over the bed and letting all her blood drain to her head. I'm huddled by the bathroom door in case I need to hide.

Now that we're all awake, the silence gets to be too much. We quote Camus until we finally acknowledge the elephant sitting in the room with us. We can't sleep anymore.

Melinda gives up hanging off the bed and curls up inside Noah's T-shirt, her whole body tucked deep inside, her arms around herself like she's cold.

Noah says, "You need to make a choice. I'll give you a chance like Chase won't. I like you a lot more."

"Not hard," I mumble.

Noah looks at me. "Shh."

"Sorry."

Melinda puts her chin on her knees.

He says, "Stop sleeping with my brother. And I'll give you a chance and we can do this for real. Not just slutty summers. Real."

Melinda has her eyes closed, rocking back and forth, and for the first time in a long time I think she looks beautiful. Not hot and not disgusting. Just beautiful.

I remember that I used to think that a lot. That I used to wonder when Bella would turn into her.

A part of me still does.

She whispers, "I love you, Noah."

I hate her again. I say, "Then what the hell were you doing with me? What did you want from me?"

She squeezes her eyes into those wrinkly slits.

"What did you want?" I say, and Noah says, "Chase," and I'm about to scream at him for trying to quiet me down when we've been so quiet for so long and I hate it I hate it and then I see he's gesturing for me to put my hands down. I was signing.

I hold my hands together and stare at them, letting them know they better not move without my permission. "I was fifteen," I say, softly. "What the fuck were you doing to me?"

She rocks back and forth. I keep expecting Noah to save her. I keep expecting him to be more of a hero and less of a curious twenty-year-old boy.

She says, "I had just been raped, Chase."

This is nothing new, this is nothing I didn't know, nothing Noah and I haven't discussed and dissected. But hearing it from her mouth is such a different word. Boys say "rape" hard and sharp to prove they'll never do it. Girls say it soft. Like it's spilled milk.

It's so much less dramatic than when she hints at it, when she hurts us with it that way.

"Loved Noah," she whispers. "But I wanted someone who would never hurt me."

I know the next thing she's about to say, and I would sell my soul or my Camus books if it would keep her from saying it.

She whispers, "I needed a child." She pulls her legs in as

they slip out of Noah's T-shirt. "Someone who would never grow out of me."

So here it is. I am sitting in this hotel room, and there are no options. I can stay a child and I will always, always, have to come back to her and that smile and those tears and that shirt and everything that shirt means, or I can grow up and never have anything to come back to.

This is where I get off.

For some reason, my response for this is to take my restless hands and pull my shoes off and throw them toward the bed. Then I'm on my feet, feeling the carpet grain with my toes and wishing I was feeling the sand. Digging in with my toes, I won't get off I won't get off I won't move you can't make me while the ocean wears the sand away.

The bass booms downstairs and I hate it, I hate it. I can't hear the rain anymore. Maybe it stopped.

"I am not your boy," I'm saying. "I'm not anybody's boy."

Noah doesn't move.

"Not yours." My voice is so hoarse, and the next thing I know I'm facing Noah and screaming, "Get off the floor! Get off the floor and take me home!"

Noah looks at me for a second, then he turns to Melinda. "You're done with him?"

She nods and wipes her eyes. "I'm done."

225

He crawls onto the bed and holds her shoulders in his hands. "Then let's try this for real, okay?"

I want to tell him *you stupid boy she is crazy and there are so many other girls around* but none of them are here and none of them are our summers. And any other girl would expect him to grow up, to be some person he doesn't want to try to be. Someone who actually follows through with the shit he says is so important. A real family man instead of a convenient one. Someone who can care about more than one person, or at least someone whose one person isn't his little brother.

So I have to just stand there, my arms around myself, pretending I'm cold.

Maybe I am cold. Maybe it's not summer anymore.

"No more," I tell her. "None."

And I know exactly what I'm giving up, and it's sitting on the bed cuddling in front of me.

"Come on," he says, and he gets to his feet. He shakes off before he touches me, like he's trying to get rid of any traces of Melinda. Like he knows I've made a switch, and if he touches me, he'll contaminate me. He'll make me a kid again. And I can't go back. I can't.

He says, "I'll take you home."

When I walk through the front door of our house, they

mob me. Both parents and every single sibling, none of them angry, all of them throwing arms around my waist, signing and speaking how happy they are that I'm home.

All except Noah, who's pulling out of the driveway, pulling back into Melinda.

EIGHTEEN

Our birthday party is on the Hathaways' porch this year. It is awkwardly comfortable without either family's oldest child here. We grill hamburgers and throw the ones we burn to the dogs. We are wasteful and extravagant and there is wrapping paper everywhere. We laugh a lot. The ocean's especially rough tonight and rumbles right along with us.

I have my guitar back out and I'm strumming along to whatever Bella feels like singing. I don't complain when she switches songs mid-line. I don't think I have the right to complain about Bella switching in the middle of something.

Looking at the guitar strap—with all their names from Noah down to Newbaby—makes me feel very small and not quite as old as I've let myself become. Which is seventeen today.

Shannon and Claudia sit with me, laughing and telling jokes, slipping marshmallows into each other's mouths. Claudia is perched on Shannon's lap. They look perfect together, like Shannon always imagined they would. It's almost insane that something, even if it's just one thing, worked out the way we thought it would.

Gideon and Lucy are both feeling way better and are going kind of stir-crazy from being restrained to the porch. **Lucy me beach go?**

Lucy birthday I sign. **Stay.**

Down at the end of the beach, someone is setting off fireworks. They send silver sparks through the dark. We only know the ocean's there because we can hear it. The whole beach looks like more sky.

Everything's smoky from the grill, the parents are all drunk, and all of us over eight have had a few beers ourselves. It's the kind of atmosphere where nothing is perfect, but it feels okay regardless—where anything could happen, but that doesn't mean you expect it to.

The last thing I expect is for Noah to roll up in the driveway with Melinda, a smile, and a gigantic raft in the shape of a seahorse.

Gideon and I grab hands and run down to greet them. Noah's standing by the car with his arms crossed, that mouthwash-commercial smile in his mouth. "Happy motherfucking birthday!" he yells.

I throw myself on him. He hugs me and laughs. He's wearing the denim jacket I gave him for Christmas.

"You came back," I say.

"Course." His eye roll gives me the feeling this is less an abbreviation of "of course" and more one of "par for the course."

"I got your message," he says softly. "Thanks."

I don't care if I'm too old to say this or think this or whatever, I love him so much. And it's okay. I hug him again.

Melinda's clinging to the car, like this isn't her house. Like she honestly doesn't think she's welcome here.

Whatever, Melinda. My brother is here.

Gideon's still pissed off at Noah—we can see it in his baby face—but he's also totally entranced by this raft. It could fit about five of him, and he's running his hands down it, feeling the spikes.

Tomorrow I tell him.

No after cake.

Ocean rough tomorrow better.

He pouts and tugs the float out of the car regardless. Melinda helps. **Lucy show?** he signs as soon as he has two free hands.

Fine.

I watch him drag it up the stairs. "So was that a present for me or for Gid?"

He shrugs. "Gid, I guess."

"So what's my present?"

"Me!" He holds his arm out. "Aaaand, this girl." He pulls Melinda toward him. "Hanging on me. And not you."

She waves at me a little, gripping Noah's arm.

It is sort of an awesome present.

"Come on," he says, slipping his arm around Melinda. "Let's go up there and pretend."

But it doesn't feel pretend. We sit on the patio and make s'mores, and it feels just like any night from a year when things were simpler: Bella's showing off her ballet, Shannon and I are hitting each other with paper plates. Nothing feels weird or abnormal or off, so it doesn't really feel like my birthday.

But we haven't had the cake yet. And something dramatic always happens before cake. So my guard isn't completely down . . . but it's pretty damn close, with Noah beside me, playing with the strap on my guitar, talking to everyone about how he and Melinda are now in a serious relationship, with Claudia smiling at Shannon in the starlight, with my parents smiling at each other. I watch.

My stomach's full of hamburgers and brothers and sisters and Hathaways. Gideon is driving me crazy, though, every second tugging my hand, telling me he wants to go down to the beach.

Raft no I tell him. **Dark.**

Raft no beach only.

He's doing the same thing to Mom and Dad, and everyone's getting so frustrated with him that Noah says, "Look, we'll take him down the beach, all right?" He takes Melinda by the hand and they sign **Come Gideon come** and he follows them, signing lots of things neither of them can either see or understand.

Eventually Claudia and Shannon and Bella and I wonder what the hell we're doing not tagging along, so, after making sure Lucy's firmly asleep under my mom's chair, we grab one another's hands and run down to the beach, shrieking. The beach is so long and we're trying to make it all the way to the water without stopping to gasp for breath, but it's so far. The stars have this extra intensity, but it's like there are not enough of them tonight. The beach is four shades darker than

usual, and everything is eerie and beautiful and temporary.
The ocean roars behind everything.

I can't believe how important this all feels. It's the birthday thing. Growing old over the course of one day always
feels to me like I'm living my last hours on earth.

Melinda and Noah are lying in the sand halfway between
the house and the beach, laughing and tickling each other.
Gideon's near them with the raft, riding it in the sand.

Claudia runs up to me and nudges my shoulder. "Tag."

"You're kidding me."

"You're *it*!" she shrieks. She runs up to Shannon and
jumps on his back. "You're it, Chase!"

I look at Noah for help. He shrugs. "What can I say?
You're it."

"I'm also twelve, apparently. . . ."

"Go play. We'll watch Gideon."

So I sprint after Claudia and Shannon to tackle them
into the sand. We run around and scream and play tag, and
eventually wrestle Melinda and Noah back to the ground,
together, and they kick at us and scream back and Shannon
calls me "soldier" but Melinda doesn't call me "Everboy."

We're lying in the sand, staring up at the sky, having
our love and our innocence. Bella sits up and says, "Where's
Gideon?"

"Noah's got him," I murmur.

Beside me, Noah sits up. I wait for him to raise his arm and point, to say, "He's right there. Gideon's right there."

He's frozen, eyes scanning the beach over and over. His fingers tighten and dig into the ground, like he's trying to steady himself with the sand.

I sit up and search the beach, the ocean. There's nobody there, just the seahorse float bobbing up and down in the breakers.

It's so far away from us. Maybe he's on it, or next to it. Maybe we just don't see him. It's so far away.

"Gideon!" I call, and nothing, ever, has sounded more futile.

But then they're all on their feet with me, and we're running toward the water, calling him with our voices and with our hands. It's so far away, the ocean's so far away, it takes us a million years to get down there. . . .

The waves are positively brutal—how did we not notice how tall they were? Stupid optical illusions of this new beach placated us, we're not used to it, and he's not used to the water. . . . He gets dizzy. . . .

Noah was supposed to be watching him, but he was with Melinda, he was watching Melinda. . . .

Noah and I are the first ones in the water, the first ones to splash over the seahorse float. *"Gideon!"* he's screaming, but I

234

can't see any of Noah except for where the stars shine off his wet hair. I'm so afraid he's going to disappear. That he'll sink underneath the water and then he'll be gone.

And I can't see any of Gideon, nothing, except a torn piece of his bathing suit snagged on the float's nozzle.

"Gideon!" everyone's screaming from the shore—Shannon sprinting back to get the parents, but he'll never make it, the beach is too long—he'll make it, but so long from now, what's the point—

Noah and I take one look at each other and we're diving, searching around with our hands and our squinted worthless eyes and our worthless ears, screaming with our mouths open under the water—he has to be here somewhere, he has to be, he cannot just disappear on us, he has to come back, he cannot just be nowhere, not now—

Gideon! We're all screaming.

"Two minutes," Noah's gasping. "It's been two minutes," and Gideon hasn't come up for air, hasn't come up for anything, hasn't bobbed out of the water to tell us it's okay, it's okay, you tried your hardest—

"Gideon!" we scream.

Why am I wet why am I cold why can't I breathe I'm out of the water they took me out of the water I don't want to be in the water why am I so cold why am I shaking is it because I'm so cold why don't I know what my fingers are saying why is it cold why is there water in my mouth why are they yelling at me.

"Hey! Chase! Chase McGill! Are you with us, soldier?"

It's Shannon. It's Shannon, holding me against the wall of the shower.

"Are you with me, soldier?" he's asking, his face covered in scratches the size of my fingernails.

People are talking. . . .

"Are you with me?" Shannon yells.

I am with no one but Noah and Camus.

Originally innocent without knowing it, we were now guilty without meaning to be.

18th SUMMER

NINETEEN

I spend a lot of time wondering if I'm going back to the beach this year. I change my mind quite a few times. Noah is steadfast from the beginning—we must come back. Months before it's even warm, he starts sending me post-cards. They're all Camus quotes. My favorite says, *"There are no more deserts. There are no more islands. Yet there is a need for them."*

Maybe there is.

"The beach isn't an island," Claudia says. "And it's not a desert." But she likes any opportunity to get me out of the house, and she especially loves traveling with me, especially when we don't bring Dad and we can choose whatever music we like. Of course, she's fourteen now, so she usually wants something dreadful. But I'll put up with dreadful for her.

"What are you going to do for college?" Claudia asks me a lot. "You can barely step past the front door."

"I'll think of something." Or I'll get over it. Isn't that what I'm doing now?

The postcard about the islands wasn't the best one Noah's sent me, but it's the one that was the most perfect and short. Some of the other ones, like the one that's sitting on my dresser at home—*When the images of earth cling too tightly to memory, when the call of happiness becomes too insistent, it happens that melancholy rises in man's heart: this is the rock's victory, this is the rock itself. The boundless grief is too heavy to bear*"—actually made me laugh a little. It's a beautiful quote, and certainly appropriate. But it's ridiculous to think that something morose as that could somehow incite me to action. That quote just reminds me of the days I get so tired that even sitting up in bed seems out of the question.

Driving down to the beach house without our parents— our parents who want so little to do with this place that they can't even bring themselves to sell it—doesn't feel as heavy as I thought it would. It's the same drive, and I don't feel any pangs in my chest with each mile away from home or anything like that. It's the same as it always was, the same as it was last year, just no father in the passenger seat. And it's not as if he's really gone. I kissed him good-bye this morning. Just like every morning. We make sure.

"When will you be back?" he asked, and I had to tell him that I didn't really know.

"But I will be back," I promised. "I will be." I kissed him again after that.

Dad's doing all right. He listens to more classical music now than he used to, and he works fewer hours, but he still talks about doing silly things like visiting national parks or taking rides in hot air balloons. We never actually do them, so he asks me to write songs about them. Which I do.

Claudia is beside me instead. She's wearing a new shirt and drumming out the beat to this song on her streaky legs. I finally convinced her to choose the spray-tan route instead of just going for it with the skin cancer, but she's too cheap to spend her money on a good place—always buying new shirts—so she's kind of orange at the moment. Noah's going to laugh. He hasn't seen us since we hit our growth spurts. Claude's pushing five eight now, and I'm probably Noah's height, though I haven't stood side to side with him in months. But we do talk. Phone calls. E-mails. The postcards. I don't tend to see him during his breaks, since I don't go over to my mom's house much. She doesn't ask me to babysit anymore.

Near the beginning of the year, in the fall, I saw Noah a lot. He made a point of stopping by whenever he was home for the weekend. Dad was always happier to see him than he expected to be, and sometimes even got a little teary when Noah left.

I don't blame Noah for what happened. None of us do. I think, for a while, he was waiting for the other shoe to drop, waiting for us to lose it and finally scream at him that we were so angry and so disappointed and we wished he'd never come home that night. He used to steal my stuff every time he came over. He wouldn't be sneaky about it, and he always took stuff that I'd be sure to notice was missing, like my favorite shirt or my toothbrush. I confronted him about it once, and he kept saying, "Why don't you tell me what you're really mad about? Why don't you tell me what the real problem is?" until I eventually told him to shut up and just stop stealing my shit. It's not as if we're still fighting about that, but that was when he stopped coming over.

I take a deep breath. I'm feeling okay about going back. Quiet, but okay. I'm feeling ready. After all, as Noah and Camus and probably Melinda—though I don't think of her much anymore—would say, *one always finds one's burden again*. The off-season hasn't made it any easier. I found my burden that night in the shower, and each of us finds it again every morning that we wake up and remember that we are four.

We haven't been four in a long time. Not since before Lucy was born. And that felt different, anyhow. Lucy doesn't fill any sort of sibling-void. We love her, but she's always felt more like our kid than our little sister, Noah and I have agreed. This makes this whole thing harder. The only thing worse than waking and realizing you're four is realizing you're fundamentally three, and it creates this awful perception that we've lost more than we actually have.

Being here without Mom and Dad will be weird, but they can't even be in the same room with each other anymore. We've lost things.

Claudia pinches her striped thighs. "I wonder if the Hathaways will be here," she says, in a snobby voice, like she's finally realizing what a pretentious name Hathaway is. It took me a while to notice this too, actually. That they sound like the type of people you'd drink tea with.

I know she hasn't talked to Shannon since my birthday— the last time Noah talked to Melinda, the last time our parents really talked to each other—but I don't know which of these were big, theatrical breaks, or which were just the only option after that night and felt so inevitable as to be boring and quiet. I'm so sensitive to these subtleties, now. I turn everything into a metaphor. I think of all things in terms of dramatic or undramatic, in finding bodies or never finding bodies.

I'm fine when we pull up to the house. I park beside Noah's car and grab our bags. Claudia rubs the back of her neck, surveying the sand, looking at all the people with their beach bags and umbrellas and bikinis. So many more people came here when the beach was smaller, or maybe they just looked more important without all the space.

"See?" I tell her, pointing to the emptiness between the groups of people. "Islands."

She sticks her tongue out at me, then I give her a little smile, which she returns. Okay, so this isn't awesome, but we can get through it. We've gotten through the past year, and we are okay. This isn't any different, just because it's here. Just because it's summer.

We go inside. Noah's in the kitchen feeding bites of cherry sno-ball to Lucy. She looks just like the pictures Mom still insists on sending every other week. Probably so I have no argument when I tell her I never see my sister. *Check your e-mail. See? There's your sister.*

And it isn't that I never see her. I drive over sometimes after school. Not very often, but when I need to, and I feel like it won't ruin anything if I do. Mom hugs me. Lucy hugs me. Five minutes of polite quiet later, I'll suddenly remember that Mom's cold, dead house is where I spent most of my childhood. And I have to remind myself that nobody's making me come. That I don't have to visit ever again if I don't want to. I have to keep reassuring myself that I don't have to go back. It's the only way I can stand it. It doesn't help that I know Mom would rather I only come over—that I only exist—when she's ready for the responsibility of caring about me. I have a hard time blaming her for that.

Now I hug Lucy, then Noah. Noah lost quite a bit of weight during those months by himself at school, and he's only just now starting to get it back. I'm pretty sure Mom's sneaking slabs of butter into everything he eats.

He smiles at me, the same Noah smile. I've learned that it's stupid to expect people to develop new, more profound smiles.

"Renters moved the furniture," I say.

"They always do. But check out the balcony. The extension looks pretty good."

Dad had to hire someone to come out here and finish the extension in September because it wasn't safe to just have the beams and nails and shit hanging around half-finished. A bigger part of me than I'd expected really regretted not finishing it ourselves.

"I'm gonna go check it out," I say, and they nod, and Lucy makes some almost-three-year-old noise of agreement.

The people Dad hired did a nice job. The boards line up way better than when we did it, the railing is stable, and they even fixed that one piece of wood into which Dad tried and failed to properly hammer about fifteen nails in a row. All in all, it looks great. Mom was right: We should have just hired professionals from the beginning. There's nothing worse than getting DIYs cleaned up. You either do it or you don't, but you have to finish. You can't stop things in the middle. I think Camus would have agreed with that.

I look up and remember why we built the extension in the first place.

You can still see only hints of it from here, but the ocean looks like it's been waiting twelve months to swallow me alive.

I throw up over the side of the balcony. People on the beach look up in disgust. I must have ruined their day.

The answer is yes: Even with the dune, you can still hear the ocean.

* * *

I can't believe I came. And I can't believe Claudia refuses to go home. What the hell are we doing here? What the hell did we expect to find?

How long are we expected to stay in this house?

Because she's three, Lucy's excused from blame, but the rest of us fail at being able to communicate, and it's somewhat scary. Especially when I consider that Claudia and I, on our own this year with Dad, have talked just fine. We compare days, we talk about our plans, we exchange I love yous. It's just adding Noah and Lucy into the equation that's making it impossible. We can't figure out how to be whole together.

I thought Claudia could do it. I thought she would be our savior. It was stupid of me to put that much weight on her shoulders, but I did. She was always the loud one, the spunky one. The one who hated inaction enough to hate philosophy. Now she just watches TV and reads magazines and texts people on her phone. I don't even know who she's texting. I don't even know what's in her head, but it isn't what's in mine.

Not that I know what's in mine.

But it's not this.

I walk around town a lot, just to get away from the silence and the ocean. I walk past where I used to work and go inside and buy some chocolate turtles. I really hope, for some reason, that it will be Joanna working the register. I can imagine it's a million years ago and I'm staring at her ass while she bends over to refill the drawers with fudge.

The girl who serves me a quarter pound of chocolate turtles doesn't look anything like her. I sit outside in the sun and eat them, slowly. I'm thinking about Melinda even though I don't want to. It's that I don't even know how to think about her anymore. The sex, not liking the sex, not needing the sex, all feels like something that touched a very different person. It's hard to imagine having sex. I guess I'll have it in college. I wonder if it'll hurt.

I can't really hear the ocean from here, but I imagine it's there. I convince myself that what I think is the wind is actually the ocean, and it's whispering.

I go out farther into the outskirts of the town where the vacationers don't go. The speech therapist's office was around here, but their office has closed. The city has started renovating some of the buildings, and it's funny how much I feel for the ones that are still unfixed, the ones that look old and rundown. They're not; they were fine last year, but they look old in comparison to their new and shiny neighbors. Like they were formed from driftwood.

I hate myself for feeling this way. It's just that, it turns out, I was right all along. There's nothing that's happened to us that these summers can't explain. I've lived a life of sun and sand and Camus and ocean, for better or for worse, and it wasn't always perfect but it was always substantial. That's a life that's not really here anymore. Even looking back, everything I did and thought was important feels stupid. Writing my name in the sand. Playing tag with Claudia. Tossing a Frisbee with Shannon. What the hell was the point of any of it, in the long run? It was all just to lead me here.

I read my age in the faces I recognized without being able to name them. I merely knew that they had been young with me and that they were no longer so.

The people I associate as being my age couldn't be older than fifteen. I want to tell them not to work at the Candy Kitchen.

There are houses here, farther from the beach, that have lawns and wind chimes and such, like they are actually places to live. I take my time to walk by them, walk through their yards. I imagine them watching me through their windows and wondering what the fuck I'm doing.

The sun gets really annoying after a few days of malcontented wandering, especially since I've been refusing sunscreen. I don't know why. I can't stand the smell, I guess. Claudia's been applying it so liberally that most of her spray tan is gone, as if the SPF will protect her from other things.

If I had lifescreen or suckscreen or deathscreen, I would give it to Claudia, no question. Claudia or Lucy. Lucy's small. Maybe they could share a bottle. Noah wouldn't take it from me, and at this point I'm not sure I should protect Noah from anything. After all, wouldn't that just be robbing him of his education?

Our favorite sno-ball place is having a sale. Two for one. Sno-balls are like sno-cones except that they're a million times better and only served here. Noah and Claudia and I used to all get different flavors, and we'd stand in a circle and spoon out bits of ours—I'd give mine to Noah, he'd give his to Claudia, she'd give hers to me. By the end we all had a little bit of each other's, as Claudia's would sneak its way onto my spoon before I could pass mine on to Noah, and Noah's would sneak onto hers, and we mingled.

These kids are all jumping up and down in front of it. Maybe they're about nine years old. Their bathing suits are shiny but grimy with sand. Water is pooling in their ears, making it hard for them to hear. Every once in a while, one of them will shout, "What?"

Laughter's absolutely pouring from their baby mouths.

I stuff my hands in the pockets of my jeans—no bathing

suit for me—and walk away. I don't know what I was expecting to find here. *Everything here suggests the horror of dying in a country that invites one to live.*

I get to the playground, where Noah and I once screamed about speech therapy. And he's there, sitting on one of the swings, scraping his heels in the dirt.

"What are you doing here?" I ask him.

"Looking for you." He reaches out and touches my arm.

I don't know what to say. Noah and I haven't talked much since we've been here. We've barely even touched in months, since the funeral, where we were overheated twins in our black jackets, the arm of my suit glued to the arm of his.

I say, "Did you want me to pick up something for dinner?"

"No, Chase. Goddamn it. I wanted to talk to you."

I breathe out slowly and tilt my head farther and farther back, slowly. My eyes are full of sky.

I say, "Talk about what?"

"The year."

I hate the year.

"How have you been?" he says, softly.

We talked every day, but we never said anything of consequence. He told me about the physics they were using in his classes, I told him about my unsurprising decision to choose, like him, a school close to home. We talked about Lucy's teeth coming in. And Camus.

I keep my head up. "Fine. You know how it is. . . ."

"I don't." He's quiet for a minute, and I hear him twisting the chain of the swing around his fingers. He says, "Because I'm not fine."

"I'm . . . sorry." God, I sound like a jerk, and a part of me wants to. A part of me wants to shut Noah out and make him feel like he's the only one who feels like shit. What's wrong with me? Why do I want him to feel alone?

"Can you sit down or something?" he says.

"Noah . . ." I walk a few steps away from him, tugging at the ends of my hair. "I don't know what I'm supposed to do. I don't even know why the fuck we came back here."

"We didn't have any other choice. We had nowhere else to go."

"God, we could have stayed home."

"We needed to be here."

"What the fuck does that mean?" I turn around and stare at him. "What the *fuck* do we need from here? What the fuck is left of this place that we haven't sucked dry? The fucking stores we've visited a million times? The restaurants where we've tried the whole menu? The ocean?"

"To be together."

"We're not together!"

He's quiet while he closes his hands into fists. "You know what? God, Chase, fuck you. This is the closest we're fucking going to get to together."

"Shut up."

"And you're supposed to be my fucking brother, and you haven't given me the fucking time of day since we've been here, and I'm just trying—"

"Yeah, well, maybe I'm just a shitty brother."

"Maybe you are."

I force a laugh. "Well, who would know better than the poster child?"

He puts his head in his hands.

Eventually, he speaks, his voice very even. "I made one mistake. One horrible fucking mistake that I would do anything in the world to undo, but that does *not* define what I've been for all of you."

He's practiced this speech. This was the speech he wanted to use when he was stealing my toothbrush.

He says, "I was the first advocate for this family. Always. I made you a fucking guitar strap, I . . . I was going to switch my major for him."

"Yeah, you talked a big fucking game about how important we were while you were running out the fucking door!

Some fucking older brother. Some fucking *Noah*, letting your baby brother drown."

This isn't fair. I don't blame Noah. But I want to, I want to hate him because it's so much easier than loving him and hugging him and crying with him and feeling and losing.

I say, "You want to talk about turning into our parents? *Shitdamn!* I hope you never grow up, you asshole! I hope you never fuck up kids of your own!"

"*I did already!*" he screams.

I just can't talk about this. I can't be here doing this. We had our time. We grieved. It's over. We're supposed to be on to acceptance now. We have to accept this. We can't keep dredging this up like the wounds are fresh just because we're here. Just because we're together. Just because we'll never be together again.

"I'm sorry," I say.

He lets out a laugh from the back of his throat. "Yeah. Everyone's sorry."

In other news, we're playing house again. I'm still the father, but now Claude's our rebellious yet lovable teenager, Luce is our baby, and Noah, who's taken over the cooking, is playing Mom. He's good at it. About as distant and ineffectual as our real thing.

"Eat more," he tells me.

"Um, backatcha."

"You look like an old man."

"God," I say. "Don't say that. Never say that again."

Noah and I aren't fighting, but this is about as meaningful a conversation as we seem able to have.

He makes steak and green beans and cuts them up into little pieces on Lucy's plate. "I wanna do it myself," she says.

"Big sharp knife," Noah says. "Not for kids." We have this bad habit of speaking to Lucy in ASL speaking patterns, which is especially strange when you consider that Noah never really learned how to sign. He switched his major to engineering.

Claudia's picking at the steak. She's made this recent fuss about turning vegetarian, but can't stick with it, so mostly she just eats meat and looks morose.

"I've been thinking . . . ," she says.

We look at her.

"Once you go to college." She gathers her hair back in her hand. "Maybe I'll ask Dad if we could move up here. It'd be nice to see the place in the off-season. Get a taste of summer all year."

Noah and I stare at her.

I guess I figured over the past week that she was just as

uncomfortable here as we are. But maybe we're the thing making her uncomfortable.

I take a sip of lemonade. "He'd never go for it."

"I know," she says. "But it couldn't hurt to ask, right?"

It could hurt *him*. I look at Noah, and we say this with our eyes. "You know what it will make him think," I say. "That you don't care. That it's not still hurting you."

She bites down on her fork, and it makes me wince. She says, "I didn't know you had to skip summers to grieve properly."

"There is no grieving properly," I mumble, borrowing a line from that therapist Dad made us see.

Claudia looks at me. "Then fuck off."

"Watch your mouth," Noah says.

We watch Lucy annihilate her green beans with her pudgy fists. The doorbell rings.

It's ridiculous the amount of panic and confusion on all our faces when we look at one another, and it just reminds me how secluded we've become. Nobody knocks on our door anymore, because no one talks to us. Why would anyone want to? We're not fun anymore.

"Get it," Noah says to me.

I go to the door, and, shit—

The brotherfucking Hathaways.

Melinda and Shannon and . . . God, even Bella.

I leave the door open because I can't be that mean, but I do just walk back inside and sit on the couch. Noah says, "Chase?"

"Hathaways," I say.

I am shutting down. I am shutting down. I am flashing back and I am shutting down.

Claudia, God bless her unfeeling little soul, takes a deep breath and goes to the door and hugs each of them in turn. "It's so good to see you," she tells them, in that voice she uses over the phone to Lucy.

Noah won't look at them, just takes Lucy out of her booster seat and plops her on the ground. "Go play," he says.

Mom must tell her this a *lot* when something interesting is about to happen, because she crosses her arms and shakes her head.

"Luce, your baby doll's crying."

"Nooooo," she cries, and she runs into her room. Bella gives her a little smile as she runs by. I scoot back on the couch to make sure I can see her play, to be sure she's safe.

"What are you doing here?" Noah asks. Quietly. So quietly. Like he doesn't really care why they're here. Doesn't really care that they're here.

The Hathaways were clearly not prepared for this question. They look at one another, then look at me.

I can't look at Shannon right now, can't remember the last time I looked at him, when he poured water all over me and called me his soldier, even though neither of us had any idea what we were fighting.

Looking at Bella just seems stupid, so I look at Melinda. Melinda who said she was watching Gideon. Melinda who acted like childhood was something she wanted to protect while she screwed me senseless and let my brother fall off the raft.

Fuck. The. Hathaways.

And Melinda, the way she's looking at me . . . it's like she knows *everything*.

Yes, I blame you. I blame all of you. I spent this whole year blaming you because I love my brother I love my brother I loved my brothers and I survive by finding something else to think about and something else to feel. It is the only way to get by. There is no grieving improperly. I blame you and I blame me and I don't want to think about it. This is how I get by. This is how I live now.

Also, it seems like if we're going to see them after so long, it should be on my birthday. For maximum dramatic effect. They should have waited. It's tomorrow. I'm sure they remember. We've all got to remember, even if no one will mention it.

"We just got here," Melinda says eventually. "Thought we'd come see how you were doing."

"Okay, you"—Noah points to Melinda—"cannot scare anyone here into bed anymore. You"—Shannon—"cannot convince my brother that college and some girl will make him happy, and you—"

"Bella hasn't done jack shit to you," Melinda says. "So shut the fuck up."

I wonder if anyone's told Noah to shut the fuck up lately. He's not living on the run anymore, not living like a gypsy, not meeting vagabonds on the streets or in bars. He's in college, going to classes. I don't know what my brother has seen, but judging by his face, he hasn't heard anything that makes him this angry in a long time. Not even me. I still can't really make Noah mad.

"We all lost something that night," she says.

I want to ask, How much is lost when you lose one person? I think Melinda might have a quote for the occasion.

"Get out of here!" Noah screams. "Get out of my house!"

Melinda is the one who meets my eye on the way out. Who looks at me and says, "We all lost something."

And she's gone. No quote. I should have known she was worthless. In the end, she was just as meaningless as everything.

Noah closes the door and comes back to the couch. "I don't care what they lost," he says, putting his arms around me. "I care that no one makes you look like that again."

I want to lean into him and hold on to him but I can't even move.

I'm sitting on my bed. It's two hours later but it feels like a million.

This is my room now, and mine only—Noah sleeps in the master bedroom. He won't be chucking stones at the window, and I don't know if I'd let him in if he did. I'm taking deep breaths so I don't have to throw myself under another shower when Claudia comes in with Noah's Camus book and says, "Listen. Just listen."

"Claude—" No.

She holds up her finger and opens the book. "'*But this cannot be shared,*'" she reads. "'*One has to have lived it.*'"

No. I pull my legs up on the bed and shake.

"'*So much solitude and nobility gives these places an unforgettable aspect,*'" she says. "'*In the warm moment before daybreak, after confronting the first bitter, black waves, a new creature breasts night's heavy, enveloping water. The memory of these days does not make me regret them, and thus I realize that they were good.*'"

I'm shaking.

"'*After so many years they still last, somewhere in this heart which finds unswerving loyalty so difficult. And I know that today, if I were to go to the deserted dune, the same sky would pour down on me its cargo of breezes and stars. These are lands of innocence.*'"

I want to climb between the pages and pull the covers over me and never have to look at her again.

She closes the book. "Yeah, it's awful that he died, Chase, and, God, it's awful that it happened here. And we've all had a really shitty year, but you have to go out there. You have to see the beach. This was your childhood. You can't let that disappear because of a really, really shitty year."

I want to say I watched my childhood drown, but the bottom line is that nobody got to watch it happen. We just splashed around after the fact.

"It's the same sky you lay under for eighteen years," she tells me. "Same ocean."

"Yeah!" I say. "Yeah, Claudia, I goddamn know it was the same ocean! The same ocean out there right now is the same one I played around in and dunked Shannon and played chicken with Noah and the same one that took my little brother on my seventeenth birthday. And I regret it! I regret all of it!"

She crosses her arms.

"Uncross your arms and put down the fucking Camus! This is our life! This is our life and it sucks, Claudia, and it will always suck from here on out and fucking here on backward but we didn't know it and I will always, always regret it."

She says, "Grow up, Chase," and closes the door.

I lay there by myself and sign **forgive you forgive you forgive you.**

TWENTY

We make a big deal out of calling it "Lucy's birthday." Not "Chase's birthday." Not "The day Gideon died." Just Lucy's birthday.

I'm eighteen now. I should be buying porn or going to a strip club with Noah or . . . what do adults do?

Instead I go for a run down the boardwalk. One of those runs where you don't save enough energy for the way back. I deplete.

I'm so sorry that it hurts every bit of my body. I'm sorry I was terrible to Bella and wouldn't look at Shannon. I'm sorry

I ever slept with Melinda. And I'm sorry I treated Melinda like shit. I'm sorry I blew Claudia off and have ignored Lucy and didn't hug Noah back and I will always, always be sorry, Gideon. I'll always be so sorry.

I keep running.

Camus and Melinda taught me that not loving was the true misfortune, and I get why now. It's not seeing this inability in yourself that's the problem. It's when you love someone who has disappeared and is no longer able to love anyone, least of all you.

It is so much more awful when you think of just how many people there are in this whole world that Gideon can't love.

I run so fast that my lungs hurt.

There are so many things I did wrong, Gideon, and so many of them were my fault and so many of them weren't. I should have learned to sign better. I should have lived with him for the last year of his life. I should have stopped looking at Noah or Claudia or Lucy to link us back together and been the one in our family who could stop hiding behind quotes and signs and actually speak, instead of the one who draped their names in a guitar strap around his shoulder and called that his support.

It's been a year, and it's been a really shitty year. Another thing the therapist didn't teach me: When you're grieving, the times you're happy are so much more tragic than the times that you aren't. Because being happy feels fake and it feels temporary and it feels meaningless. And hating being happy is a shitty way to live. And I don't feel happy now. I don't think I'll ever feel happy the way I did before he died, but I never want to feel happy the way I have after he died either. A shadow of the real. That's Plato, not Camus. I want Camus. But I want to feel happy like me. Not like Camus. I want to feel like me despite the people who are here and shouldn't be and the ones who aren't but I can't figure out why.

I want to be Chase who ate a sno-ball and Chase who hugged Gideon and Chase who fucked Melinda and Chase who everything in the whole world. I have to be more than just who I am in this second. I *have* to be, because right now I'm not . . .

I'm not anything.

I stop to breathe. I'm at the end of the boardwalk.

The thing I neglected to take into account about the boardwalk is that it ends at the ocean.

And here it is. A mile or so and three hundred and sixty-five days from where Gideon died, but it's the same ocean.

Goddamn it, the sun's out and there are children playing

and it is beautiful. It's sparkling and it's gorgeous. And it killed my brother.

And this indifferent, silent universe, it sucks for making Gideon deaf, it sucks harder for taking him away and hardest for doing it on my birthday, but it gave me Gideon in the first place. It gave me Noah and made him run and gave me Mom and Dad and made them break up and gave me Claudia and Lucy and Melinda and Shannon and Bella, for a little while. It gave me summers and childhood and it took the childhood away, but there were summers before I was born, and there will be summers after I die, and after he died, and that's what I believe in. I believe in these summers.

They did happen. I was there. They will always have happened.

There is no going back, so fuck you, universe. There is nothing you can do to take back the fact that you gave me everything I need to get by.

So fuck you.

And thank you.

Things might be very different next year.

Some things will not ever change. My childhood is preserved in photo albums, in sand castles, in *The Stranger*, and in every single fucking one of my siblings. Every single one.

To nobody, because Gideon cannot hear me, I say, "I'm sorry I wasn't watching."

I love you I sign. **Not same. Never same. I love you.**

There is no past tense in sign language, not really. It's all about positioning. About where you are right now.

Eighteen of these summers behind me give me the energy to run home.

I run straight to Noah and give him the biggest hug of my life.

We don't talk.

We still don't know what to say. Maybe we never will. Maybe it isn't in us. Neither of us is going to grow up to be a motivational speaker.

But we can grow up to be brothers.

I feel my hands on his shoulders and his hands on mine, and it's okay. There's a tiny part of this that's okay. The smallest glimmer of fine is trapped somewhere between our bodies.

"You're not a bad brother," we say together.

Then I go outside and flop down in the sand beside Claudia. My chest is heaving, and my shirt is stuck down with sweat. I'm disgusting. Good thing this is my shirt and not Noah's.

She looks at me and wisely makes no comment that I'm on the beach, that I'm facing the ocean, that I'm not running away. She does give me a sly smile, though. "Want to go swimming?"

I laugh. "Maybe not quite yet."

Lucy's wandering around in the sand in front of us. I say, "Where's Noah?" I suspect he went for a run after our not-talk. That was pretty draining, and he probably needed to get away.

But she points over to the house. "There." And there he is, perched on the steps between the house and the sand, watching the ocean too. I wonder when he was first able to look at it, and realize I haven't been watching him very closely. I should. Noah needs our help.

"It's been a shitty year," Claudia says.

"That it has."

"Are you okay?"

I lean onto my knees. *"'His joys have been sudden and merciless, as has been his life. One realizes that he is born of this country where everything is given to be taken away. In that plenty and profusion life follows the sweep of great passions, sudden, exacting, and generous. It is not to be built up, but to be burned up. Stopping to think and becoming better are out of the question.'"*

She looks at me for a minute.

"I'm getting there," I say. "Or I'm burning up."

I guess that in the end it's true. *Innocence needs sand and stones.* And it doesn't matter how that makes me feel.

Besides, right now, all I feel is a little cold in the sunset.

The ocean crashes with the noise of a bowling alley as another wave hits the sand. Lucy is toddling toward the water.

Before I can get up, before I can open my mouth—either to tell her to stay or tell her to swim as far and as fast as she can before she can't—Noah sprints from behind us and grabs her, his arms around her little body. Keeping her still. Keeping her from running away.

How far is too far?
Don't miss

Break

by Hannah Moskowitz

one

THE FIRST FEELING IS EXHILARATION.

My arms hit the ground. The sound is like a mallet against a crab.

Pure fucking exhilaration.

Beside me, my skateboard is a stranded turtle on its back. The wheels shriek with each spin.

And then—oh. *Oh,* the pain.

The second feeling is pain.

Naomi's camera beeps and she makes a triumphant noise in her throat. "You *totally* got it that time," she says. "Tell me you got it."

I hold my breath for a moment until I can say, "We got it."

"You fell like a bag of mashed potatoes." Her sneakers make bubble gum smacks against the pavement on her way to me. "Just . . . splat."

So vivid, that girl.

Naomi's beside me, and her tiny hand is an ice cube on my smoldering back.

"Don't get up," she says.

I choke out a sweaty, clogged piece of laughter. "Wasn't going to, babe."

"Whoa, you're bleeding."

"Yeah, I thought so." Blood's the unfortunate side effect of a hard-core fall. I pick my head up and shake my neck, just to be sure I can. "This was a definitely a good one."

I let her roll me onto my back. My right hand stays pinned, tucked grotesquely under my arm, fingers facing back toward my elbow.

She nods. "Wrist's broken."

"Huh, you think?" I swallow. "Where's the blood?"

"Top of your forehead."

I sit up and lean against Naomi's popsicle stick of a body and wipe the blood off my forehead with my left hand. She gives me a quick squeeze around the shoulders, which is basically as affectionate as Naomi gets. She'd probably shake hands on her deathbed.

She takes off her baseball cap, brushes back her hair, and replaces the cap with the brim tilted down. "So what's the final tally, kid?"

Ow. Shit. "Hold on a second."

She waits while I pant, my head against my skinned knee. Colors explode in the back of my head. The pain's almost electric.

"Hurt a lot?" she asks.

I expand and burst in a thousand little balloons. "Remind me why I'm doing this again?"

"Shut up, you."

I manage to smile. "I know. Just kidding."

"So what hurts? Where's it coming from?"

"My brain."

She exhales, rolling her eyes. "And your brain is getting these pain signals from where, sensei?"

"Check my ankles." I raise my head and sit up, balancing on my good arm. I suck on a bloody finger and click off my helmet. The straps flap around my chin. I taste like copper and dirt.

I squint sideways into the green fluorescence of the 7-Eleven. No one inside has noticed us, but it's only a matter of time. Damn. "Hurry it up, Nom?"

She takes each of my sneakered feet by the toe and moves it carefully back and forth, side to side, up and down. I close my eyes and feel all the muscles, tendons, and bones shift perfectly.

"Anything?"

I shake my head. "They're fine."

"Just the wrist, then?"

"No. There's something else. It-it's too much pain to be just the wrist. . . . It's somewhere. . . ." I gesture weakly.

"You seriously can't tell?"

"Just give me a second."

Naomi never gets hurt. She doesn't understand. I think she's irritated until she does that nose-wrinkle. "Look, we're not talking spinal damage or something here, right? Because I'm going to feel really shitty about helping you in your little mission if you end up with spinal damage."

I kick her to demonstrate my un-paralysis.

She smiles. "Smart-ass."

I breathe in and my chest kicks. "Hey. I think it's the ribs."

Naomi pulls up my T-shirt and checks my chest. While she takes care of that, I wiggle all my fingers around, just to check. They're fine—untouched except for scrapes from the pavement. I dig a few rocks from underneath a nail.

"I'm guessing two broken ribs," she says.

"Two?"

"Yeah. Both on the right."

I nod, gulping against the third feeling—nausea.

"Jonah?"

I ignore her and struggle to distract myself. Add today to the total, and that's 2 femurs + 1 elbow + 1 collarbone + 1 foot + 4 fingers + 1 ankle + 2 toes + 1 kneecap + 1 fibula + 1 wrist + 2 ribs.

= 17 broken bones.

189 to go.

Naomi looks left to the 7-Eleven. "If we don't get out of here soon, someone's going to want to know if you're okay. And then we'll have to find another gross parking lot for next time."

"Relax. I'm not doing any more skateboard crashes."

"Oh, yeah?"

"Enough with the skateboard. We've got to be more creative next time, or your video's gonna get boring."

She makes that wicked smile. "You okay to stand?" She takes my good hand and pulls me up. My right wrist dangles off to the side like the limb of a broken marionette. I want to hold it up, but Naomi's got me in a death grip so I won't fall.

My stomach clenches. I gasp, and it kills. "Shit, Nom."

"You're okay."

"I'm gonna puke."

"Push through this. Come on. You're a big boy."

Any other time, I would tease her mercilessly for this comment. And she knows it. Damn this girl.

I'm upright, but that's about as far as I'm going to go. I lean against the grody wall of the Laundromat. "Just bring the car around. I can't walk that far."

She makes her hard-ass face. "There's nothing wrong with your legs. I'm not going to baby you."

My mouth tastes like cat litter. "Nom."

She shakes her hair and shoves down the brim of her cap. "You really do look like crap."

She always expects me to enjoy this part. She thinks a boy who likes breaking bones has to like the pain.

Yeah. Just like Indiana Jones loves those damn snakes.

I do begging eyes.

"All right," she says. "I'll get the car. Keep your ribs on."

This is Naomi's idea of funny.

She slouches off. I watch her blur into a lump of sweatshirt, baseball cap, and oversize jeans.

Shit. Feeling number four is worry. Problems carpet bomb my brain.

What am I going to tell my parents? How is this setting a good example for Jesse? What the hell am I doing in the grossest parking lot in the city on a Tuesday night?

The feeling that never comes is regret.

There's no room. Because you know you're three bones closer.

Hannah Moskowitz grew up in Silver Spring, Maryland, but mostly in Chase's beach house in Bethany Beach, Delaware. Her first novel, *Break*, was a 2010 ALA Popular Paperback for Teens. She loves your e-mails. She's a student at the University of Maryland. Visit her at untilhannah.com or hannahmosk.blogspot.com.

ACKNOWLEDGMENTS

This book is a thank-you letter. Now you know.

To Anica Rissi, for loving this book from the start and pushing it to its limit. To Brendan Deneen, Suzie Townsend, and the entire FinePrint team for welcoming me when I was more of an idea than a writer. To every single person who read *Break*, every single freaking one of you, who may never know how much you've helped me. To the Musers, who couldn't possibly ever know. To the Washington, D.C., and Providence, RI, Deaf communities—I hope I have made you proud. To Albert Camus—*merci*—and Jenn Lloyd, the best teachers I have ever known. To Christopher, always. To Seth, Alex, Emma, Galen. Mom, Dad, and Abby. And you. For carrying me here. It has been sweeter than I can ever say.

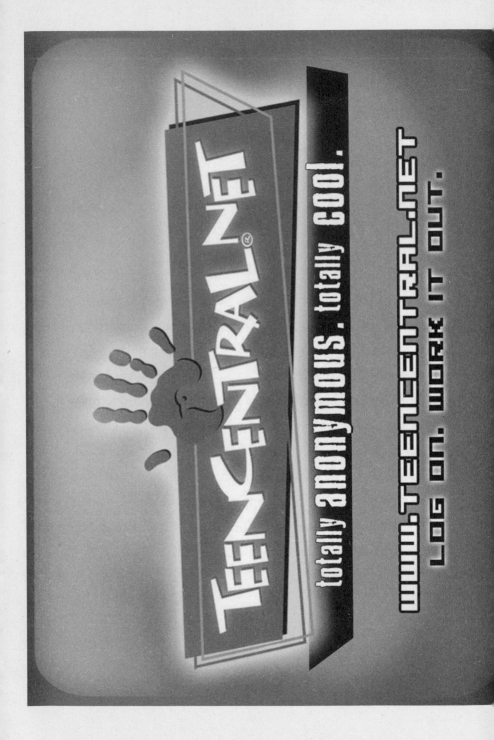